What others are

"…Ann Simas seamlessly in
SPIRIT] with a budding rom
– Stacie Theis, BeachBoun

MW01226320

"I really loved [CHLOE'S SPIRIT]. It ended way too soon."
– SheriO (Reader, Amazon Kindle)

"…you won't want to put [FIRST STAR] down."
– lfb68 (Reader, Amazon Kindle)

"[FIRST STAR]…is Romantic Suspense at its best."
– Linda Strong (Reader, Amazon Kindle)

"BLESSED ARE THE EAGLES should be made into a movie, it was that good."
– Dee Matt (Reader, Amazon Kindle)

"[BLESSED ARE THE EAGLES] is a gripping story..."
– Bella's Blog (Reader, Amazon Canada)

"[BLESSED ARE THE EAGLES] had so many of the elements that I adore in fiction! A mystery (or several) to solve, hidden threats, mystical paranormal elements that kept me guessing and eager for more, as well as a pair of protagonists who are certainly NOT cookie cutter characters."
– Whatcha Readin'? (Reader, Amazon Kindle)

"If I was ever to write a book involving steamy passages, LOOSE ENDS would be the template for style and dialogue. [Simas] is a breath of sultry air."
– Dolores Walker (Reader, Ottawa, Canada)

"[LOOSE ENDS] kept me reading late into the night…thank you Ann Simas for an excellent read."
– Michelle Turner (Reader, Amazon United Kingdom)

"[Ann Simas] did a great job blending the forensic and investigative elements [in DRESSED TO DIE]."
– Lt. Mike Hurley (Ret.), Director, Oregon State Crime Lab, Springfield

"HOLY SMOKE…is awesome! The depth of subject is something this author is extremely good at."
– Josephine Musumeci (Reader, Amazon Kindle)

"Wow!! Finished reading HEAVEN SENT a couple of weeks ago and it is still rumbling around in my brain."
– Luanne Costanzo, Reader (via Ann Simas, Author Facebook page)

"[HEAVEN SENT] is a truly remarkable story filled will love, faith, determination and suspense."
– Niki Driscoll (Reader, Amazon Kindle)

"[HEAVEN SENT] is a wonderful, scary, and uplifting book."
– Christine Holmes (Reader, Amazon United Kingdom)

"I give [SANTA'S HELPER] 6 Candi Kisses because 5 is not enough."
– Candace Fox, Candi's Books & Reviews

"SLICED TO DIE…has characters you like, is easy to read, and hard to put down! This book does not disappoint…[Simas's] wit, imagination and writing skills are amazing."
– Rebecca Hunter (Reader, Amazon Kindle)

"[PENITENCE]…leaves you in suspense right up until the end."
– Gary Wolfe (Reader, Amazon Kindle)

"[BLACK MOON RISING is] a heart pumping, rush of adrenaline story. You won't be disappointed…it has everything you can imagine: romance, adventure, mystery, and mayhem all rolled into one spectacular book!"
– Jessica Mitchell (Reader, Amazon Kindle)

"[BLACK MOON RISING] was holy wow."
– Starswarlover (Reader, Amazon Kindle)

"Ann Simas has struck gold [with BURIED TO DIE). It's a great read."
    – Chuck Wallace, Reader (via Ann Simas Facebook page)
"I like everything about [FRUITYCAKES]. It gave me such a warm feeling and it also made me laugh."
    – Annette (Reader, BookBub)
"Loved 'HERE AND GONE' couldn't hardly put it down, but my animals and husband needed to eat."
    – Nora Levenhagen (Paperback Reader, Amazon)
"[HERE AND GONE] just pulls you in and you just keep reading and reading to find out what happens next."
    – Jamie Kurp (via Candid Book Reviews)
"[HERE AND GONE] proves to be stuffed with danger and drama…[Ann Simas] has given her finest in this one, keeping us engaged through every bit."
    – Denise Van Plew (Reader, Amazon Kindle)
"Love, love, loved [HERE AND GONE]! Hoping for a sequel!"
    – Gayle J. Brown (Reader, via Facebook)
"Death threats, crooked cops, sexual tension, dead bodies, crop circles and a cliffhanger all wrapped up in a satisfying thriller [in QUILTED TO DIE]!"
    – Kindle Reader (Reader, Amazon Kindle)
"You may need tissues for [ANGELS ON THE ROOFTOP]."
    – Christine Campbell (Reader, Amazon Kindle)
"[DECK THE GNOMES] is a fun entertaining holiday romance that had me laughing out loud at times."
    – Brenda M. (Reader, Amazon Kindle)
"BACK-DOOR SANTA is such a cute and funny romance novel. [Simas] has a way with her characters that I never really see that much in other books."
    – Jessica Mitchell (Reader, Amazon Kindle)
"I loved, loved, loved [TAKEN TO DIE]! It took me a month to get started reading this book because I knew I wouldn't want it to end. I love the Grace Gabbiano series so much and can hardly wait for the next installment."
    – cocogib (Reader, Amazon Kindle)
"[In JINGLE BELL CLOCK] there's magic in the air and a mystery to be solved!"
    – Emily Pennington (Reader, Amazon Kindle)
"[REINDEER BLITZ is] something a little bit different but very entertaining. A perfect festive treat to curl up with.
    – Amanda (UK Reader, Amazon Kindle)
"You are not going to want to put this book down! DISAPPEARING ACT is a page turner from the beginning of the story until the happily-ever-after at the end."
    – hmg_vermont (Reader, Amazon Kindle)
"[HOLLY JOLLIES is] funny, sweet, romantic, cute, and a feel-good read."
    – M Blandon (Reader, Amazon Kindle)
"[YULE LOGE] is an easy, fun read…about relationships, family, and commitment."
    – gsw (Reader, Amazon Kindle)
"[RUN OR DON'T has] suspense, drama, danger, twists, turns, very twisted villains, murder, and romance. I would recommend."
    – Babs (Reader, Amazon Kindle)
"[FRAMED TO DIE] is a fascinating story with twists and turns…highly recommended!"
    – Gary Wolfe (Reader, Amazon Kindle)
"I love the development of the peripheral characters and the Gabbiano family. Read [HIDDEN TO DIE]…you won't be disappointed!"
    – cocogib (Reader, Amazon Kindle)

Books by Ann Simas...

Afterstories

Chloe's Spirit[†]   First Star[†]
Chloe's Spirit Afterstories   First Star Afterstories

Stand-Alones

Blessed Are the Eagles[†]
Loose Ends
Heaven Sent
Black Moon Rising
Fortune's Cookie *(May 2023)*

Fossil, Colorado Books

Here and Gone
Disappearing Act
Run or Don't
Now or Never

Grace Gabbiano Mysteries

Dressed to Die
Sliced to Die
Buried to Die
Quilted to Die
Taken To Die
Praying to Die
Framed to Die
Hidden to Die

Andi Comstock Supernatural Mysteries

Holy Smoke
Penitence
Angel Babies
Hellfire
The Wrong Wicca
Last Rites

Christmas Valley Romances

Santa's Helper   Candy Cane Lane
Let It Snow   FruityCakes
Sleigh Bride   Angels on the Rooftop
Deck the Gnomes   Back-Door Santa
Jingle Bell Clock   Reindeer Blitz
Holly Jollies   Yule Loge

Sugar Plum Creek Holiday Books

Merry Witchy Christmas *(November 2022)*
Stupid Cupid *(February 2023)*

Short Story Collection

All's Well

[†]RWA Golden Heart Finalists

MERRY WITCHY CHRISTMAS

ANN SIMAS

MAGIC
MOON
PRESS

MERRY WITCHY CHRISTMAS

November 2022

Merry Witchy Christmas is a work of fiction. Names, characters, places, and incidents are either the product of the author's imagination or are used fictitiously. Any resemblance to actual persons, living or dead, or events described herein, is entirely coincidental.

ISBN 979-8-9860750-0-6 (print book)

Magic Moon Press · Eugene, OR 97408

Editing by Nancy Jankow

Printed in U.S.A.
092822/11pthyph
KP 8986075006

Christmas waves a magic wand
over this world, and behold,
everything is softer and more beautiful.
– Norman Vincent Peale

Don't get your tinsel in a tangle.
– Unknown

CHAPTER 1

HALLOWEEN NIGHT, TRICK-OR-TREATING

Maureen O'Rourke left her brother's house at 5:30 on the dot.

She heard Clancy hollering after them that little kids shouldn't be taken out so late.

Mo shouted back that trick-or-treating was no fun if you did it when the sun was still shining.

Mo, one, Clancy, zip.

Her charges were Clancy's kids — three-year-old Jett and five-year-old Kenzie — so maybe she should've listened to him. On the other hand, there was no way Halloween was as much fun during daylight hours.

Mo, two, Clancy, still zip.

During the workweek, Maureen, otherwise known as Auntie Mo, was the kids' babysitter. Tonight, she was also their trick-or-treat guide. Not that they were going to do more than circle the block, but that didn't matter. Kenzie and Jett were so excited, they'd been practically bouncing off the walls all day.

Jett looked adorable in his dragon costume and Kenzie had begged to be Twinkerbell (so named by Jett), up to and including a "magic" wand, complete with a dozen colorful ribbon streamers.

Mo had tried and tried to convince Jett that the fairy's name was Tinkerbell, but Jett was having none of it. From here until infinity, Peter Pan's sidekick would be Twinkerbell in the O'Rourke house (or Twinkabell, in Jett's parlance).

Since her niece and nephew no longer had a mother in the picture, Grammy had sewn the costumes. She'd started a month ahead of time, in case she encountered any glitches.

Mo smiled. Planning ahead for extenuating circumstances was *so* Sally O'Rourke.

"Okay," Mo said to the two little ones, "I want you to walk in front of me and hold each other's hands. We'll go to the corner and cross the street, then come back and go around this block, finishing up on this side of the street. Got it?"

They nodded up at her with expectant expressions and twinkling eyes. Even so, Mo wasn't convinced that Jett understood the words coming out of her mouth, or worse, that he even cared.

She bent down and looked him right in his beautiful green eyes. "Jett, you listen to me and Kenzie, okay?"

He nodded again and sealed the deal with his cute little smile.

"We'll probably be gone around an hour, or maybe a little longer." She propped her hands on her hips. "Just so you know, I'm not going carry you, if you get tired."

"That's okay, Auntie Mo," Jett said. "I can walk. I pwomise."

"Good boy." She patted his dragon head. "Let's go."

Jett took off running, leaving them in his three-year-old dust.

"Jett, what did Auntie Mo just tell you?" Kenzie screamed after him.

Mo rolled her eyes, knowing her nephew had no intention of answering.

He didn't bother to curb his speed, either, but because he was only three, he had short legs. She and Kenzie caught up with him in no time.

Mo stepped on his dragon tail, which brought him to a standstill pretty darned quick. "Wanna go back home?"

"Nooooo!" he yelled at her.

"Gotta follow Auntie Mo's rules," Kenzie lectured with her wand dancing.

"Whyyyyy?" he wailed.

"Because," Maureen said, "I'm the boss when you're in my care. What I say goes."

He stomped his dragon foot against the sidewalk. "I need candy."

"Are you ready to mind me?"

He smiled that cute little smile of his again, nodded, then spun around (whapping her ankle with his tail) and immediately began to run again.

"He's hopeless," Kenzie called over her shoulder as she tore off after him.

Maureen reached him first. She scooped him up before he stepped into the street.

"I thought you weren't gonna carry me!" he said, still smiling.

"I have a good mind to turn around and carry you home. Kenzie and I can trick-or-treat without you." She looked both ways before they crossed the street.

Tears welled in his big green eyes. "Nooooo!"

She set him down on the opposite corner, blocking other trick-or-treaters, who stared at him like he'd just been incarcerated in the Juvenile Delinquent Funny Farm. "Here's the deal, Jett. If you run away one more time, I'm taking you directly back to your house. There will be no discussion, and no negotiations, period. Do I make myself clear?"

This time, he nodded solemnly and took his sister's hand. "I fowgot what I'm s'pposed to say when the peoples open their doors."

"Trick-or-treat," Kenzie informed him. "And when they give you the candy, you say thank you." She sighed. "I hope no one asks us to do tricks."

"Why?" Jett asked. "I like twicks."

Kenzie shook her head in disgust. "You're impossible!"

He nodded vigorously, tugging his sister up the sidewalk to the first house.

"I'll wait right here for you," Mo called after them. Maybe Clancy had been right, after all. Jett had missed his afternoon nap. By bedtime, he'd be a raving nightmare. That made her grimace. Hell! He was already a nightmare, albeit a sweet one, and it was only five-thirty.

The two of them came skipping back to her.

"We gots candy," Jett cried. "I love Baby Wuths!"

Mo belatedly realized she hadn't told the kids they couldn't devour all the candy dropped into their trick-or-treat pumpkins. "I know you do, sweetie, but you still can't eat every piece tonight. You'll be puking your guts out, if you do."

He looked sorrowfully at his half-size Baby Ruth. "I don't like fwowing up." When he looked up at her again, he asked, "Can I eat this?"

Mo caved in immediately. "Yes, but don't eat any more unless I say so."

"C'mon, Jett. We've got more houses to trick-or-treat." This time, it was Kenzie dragging Jett behind her.

Finally, they made the end of the block and crossed the street again. Mo said again, "We'll head around the block, then we'll do your side of the street, and after that we'll be done."

"Will we gets enough candy?" Jett asked with a worried frown.

"Believe me, you'll have plenty," Mo assured him.

When they reached the other end of the backside of their block, both kids stared down the curvy sidewalk leading to the last house. Set back from the street, it had purple lights shining on the front door.

"Why does it gots puwple lights?" Jett asked.

"It's a mood thing," Mo said.

"What's a mood?" he persisted.

"Remember when we saw houses with orange lights?"

He nodded.

"Well, purple is a Halloween color, too. It sets the mood of the day, and Halloween is a fun but creepy day."

"What's cweepy?" Jett asked.

Mo thought for a second. "Scary." She raised her hands as if they were claws and snarled at him, which made him giggle.

"You awen't scawy, Auntie Mo!" He looked back at the house, but still hesitated.

"C'mon, Jett," Kenzie said. "It's just a house with purple lights."

He wasn't convinced. "Will you walk us up, Auntie Mo?"

"Sure."

Jett shuffled along, clutching Kenzie's hand so hard she yelled, "Ouch."

Together, they climbed the three steps to the porch and rang the doorbell.

A moment later, a real, live witch cackled at them, "Happy Halloween, kiddies!"

Jett screamed, stumbled backward, and would've tumbled off the porch if Mo hadn't caught him. He immediately began to cry.

The witch reached out to him and he screamed again.

She looked at Maureen. "I'm sorry, I didn't mean to scare him. I was trying to stay in witch mode."

"He's tired," Mo said.

Jett wiggled out of Mo's arms and flew off the porch. "She wants to eat me!" he screamed.

"No she doesn't," Mo assured him, hurrying after him.

The witch put two pieces of candy into Kenzie's pumpkin, and said, "I love your Tinkerbell costume."

"I'm not Tinkerbell," Kenzie informed her, grinning. "I'm Twinkerbell." She lifted her magic wand and swung it around.

The witch laughed, delighted by Kenzie's response. "I have a dog named Twinkle."

Kenzie halted her wand-waving. "You do?"

The witch nodded.

Jett continued to scream, "She wants to eat me!"

Clancy's next-door neighbors were coming up the walk. Katie Rao had started out with her four kids on the same path Mo, Kenzie, and Jett had taken.

"Will you take Kenzie, so she can finish trick-or-treating?" Mo asked. "I need to take Jett home."

"Sure," Katie said, frowning. "What's wrong with him?"

"Apparently, he doesn't like witches."

"But witches are part of Halloween," Katie said, glancing at the door. Her four kids uttered the magic words in unison, "Trick-or-treat!"

"She wants to eat me!" Jet screamed one more time.

Mo shrugged and hauled it as fast as she could down the sidewalk and around the block to Jett's house.

Clancy O'Rourke cursed a blue streak. Why couldn't the trick-or-treaters ignore his house? He hadn't left the damned porch light on, had he? All he wanted was an hour of peace and quiet at the end of what had been an incredibly shitty day.

The fact that it was Halloween made the day even worse.

Truth be told, he hated Halloween.

Mindy had walked out on him and the kids two years ago today. She'd filed for divorce, said she didn't want custody, joint or otherwise, or anything out of the house, except her clothing and what little jewelry she had. That said, she'd left her wedding rings behind. After a year, Clancy had sold them and used the money to open bank accounts for Kenzie and Jett.

He had no idea where his ex was now, nor did he care. In his mind, a woman who walked away from her children was less than nothing to him.

The front door flew open.

He jumped up, startled because Jett was screaming. "What's wrong?"

"The witch scawed me!" he wailed. "She wants to eat me!"

"Jett," Mo said, trying to pry his arms away from the stranglehold he had on her neck. "I told you, the witch does *not* want to eat you."

"She gots pointy teeth!" he insisted.

"They were fake."

"Nooooo!"

Clancy snatched his son out of his sister's arms. "Listen to me, my little dragon. There's no such thing as witches."

"Yesssss! She wants to eat me!" he screamed again.

Clancy looked at his sister. "Where does this 'witch' live?"

"Just around the corner, in the house that was for sale for so long last year. She's fixed it up really nice."

Jett smacked his small hands against his dad's cheeks to steer his attention back to him. "Witches awa mean,

Daddy. She pwob'ly alweady eated Kenzie."

No matter what Clancy said to his son, no matter how many reassurances he uttered, Jett carried on like the Hounds of Hell, plus some, were after him. Finally, he said, "How about a piece of candy?"

"Nooooo!"

That's when Clancy realized he had no choice but to deal with the witch before she cooked Jett in her cauldron. He set his sobbing dragon-son on the sofa and said to Maureen, "Will you get him into his pajamas?"

"Sure." She watched as he headed for the door. "Where are you going?"

"To take down a witch."

"Clancy, don't do anything you're going to regret! Honest, she didn't do or say anything to Jett that was bad! He's tired and over-reacting, that's all."

Clancy slammed the door on her last word and headed down the block, his strides long and purposeful. With every step he took, his anger increased. No damned witch was going to eat his kid, by God!

"Hi, Daddy," Kenzie said, waving as he approached.

Clancy lurched to a stop. He'd completely forgotten about his daughter, with all Jett's screaming. "Hi, Kenz. How's the trick-or-treat going?"

"My punkin is completely full. Our neighbors really had a lot of candy to give away."

He stooped to hug her, straightened, and walked away, again with long, angry strides.

"Where are you going, Daddy?" she called after him.

"To take down a witch," he said again.

"Uh-oh," Kenzie said.

"What's wrong, sweetie?" Katie asked.

"Daddy's going over to ream that witch a new one."

CHAPTER 2

AFTER TRICK-OR-TREATING

Clancy barreled up the porch steps, scowling at the purple lights shining down on him. He pounded on the door, and when no one answered, he put his finger against the doorbell and left it there. Still, no one opened the door.

By then, he was furious and started pounding on the door again. He was still pounding when the next batch of trick-or-treaters climbed the porch steps.

"Hey, mister, could you move over, please?" asked a kid he didn't recognize. "We want to trick-or-treat the witch."

Startled, Clancy looked down. His hand fell to his side and he wondered what the hell was wrong with him. "Sorry," he said, stepping aside. A moment later, he headed back home, lecturing himself about being an idiot.

At the corner, he took a moment to look back. The group of kids at the witch's door were laughing at something she'd said. So, she *was* there, probably hiding because he'd been such a jackass, pounding on her door like some kind of lunatic.

Maybe Mo was right. Maybe Jett had over-reacted.

Either that, or his kid could read people better than Auntie Mo managed it.

Regardless, he'd deal with this after he calmed down and had a good night's sleep. Tomorrow or the next day, he'd come back and give the witch hell for scaring the bejesus out of his kid.

Avery Lark peered out the peephole again, wondering about the man who'd pounded on her door. Eyeing him through the eye-hole, he'd looked so pissed, she jumped to the logical conclusion he was the father of the little boy who'd started crying when she said, *Happy Halloween, kiddies!* Was she really that terrifying? None of the other trick-or-treaters had cried or screamed that she was going to eat them.

The man and his family must live in the neighborhood. It hadn't been that long since the adorable little dragon had been at her door. Even though she'd moved in almost a year ago, she didn't get out much, and basically knew none of her neighbors. Remodeling and updating the house had taken most of her spare time. Work and sleep had taken up what was left of her days.

She took a step back.

Seconds later, her doorbell chimed. Avery looked through the peephole to make sure it wasn't Ticked-Off Guy, trying to trick her with one short ring. She breathed a sigh of relief.

Kids. Thank God!

"Did you kill the witch, Daddy?" Kenzie asked, frowning fiercely at him. She clutched her overflowing pumpkin in one hand and her wand in the other and both hands were in fists on her hips.

"No," Clancy barked. "Was I supposed to?"

"You looked so mad, I thought that's what you were gonna do."

He stared down at his daughter, who had tears streaming down her face. "What's wrong with you?"

"Jett's just a kid," she sobbed. "He's only been trick-or-treating once before, and that was on our side of the street."

"And?"

"He doesn't know about witches, and that witch was really nice." She glanced at her aunt. "She actually looked like a witch, didn't she, Auntie Mo?"

"She sure did," Mo said, glaring at her brother. "What's got your knickers in a knot, anyway?"

"I had a rotten day. All I wanted to do while you were gone was relax, but the doorbell kept ringing."

"Poor wittle you," she said by way of offering commiseration.

"Stuff it, Mo."

"I'd like to stuff you...in a closet or something. That poor woman is probably wondering if you escaped from the psych ward, or something worse."

"She never opened her door."

"Good for her."

"Some trick-or-treaters came up while I was having my temper tantrum. I was on my way home, but turned back to look. She said something that made them laugh."

"Gosh," Maureen said, going for disingenuous, "she sounds really awful."

"Kenzie, go get your jammies on," Clancy said to his daughter.

"I want to be Twinkerbell for a little longer."

"You can be Twinkerbell tomorrow. All day, since it's Saturday."

She put her hands back on her hips and said, "You're no fun, you know that?"

"He sure isn't," Mo agreed. She extended her hand to Kenzie. "C'mon, I'll help you get out of your costume." She stuck her tongue out at her brother. "Scrooge!"

Avery Lark turned off her outside purple lights at eight o'clock. The candy was gone and she was exhausted. Who knew saying *Happy Halloween, kiddies* dozens and dozens of times could wear a person out? Still and all, it had been a fun night, if you didn't count the little dragon.

She pulled off her witches hat and plopped it in the candy bowl. After that, she shed the black robe and let it lie where it fell. Next, she headed to her bedroom and the master bath, where she discarded her undergarments and removed her pointy teeth and faux fingernails before she stepped into the shower. She scrubbed the green stuff off her face first, then shampooed her hair. Assured the green goop was gone, and her long, dark hair was clean, she soaped good, rinsed the conditioner out of her hair and the soap off her body, and shut off the water. She cleaned the glass next, then dried and stepped out of the shower.

Toweling her hair, she turned to look at the two shower heads.

A wild thought intruded. Would Ticked-Off Guy like showering with her?

Avery grunted and turned back to finish towel-drying her hair. Where had *that* thought come from? She didn't know Ticked-Off Guy. She had no idea what he was like when he wasn't so obviously furious.

Heck, she didn't even know his name.

But he was good-looking.

And he had a powerful physique.

And two cute kids.

Not to mention, an enchanting demeanor. Not!

"Enchanting, my ass!" she muttered, pulling on her pajamas. He was so rude, he made ogres look polite.

And he had a wife, too, so get over it.

CHAPTER 3

TWO DAYS AFTER HALLOWEEN

Avery stewed over the Ticked-Off Guy for two days. Who was he, and why had she been so afraid to open her door to him?

Then she'd stew some more, wondering about his wife, the pretty woman who'd brought the kids trick-or-treating. Avery might have been a lot of things, but she didn't poach husbands from their wives.

While she fixed her lunch on Sunday, she tried to decide why knowing his name would make a difference.

The only thing she could come up with was that she could look up his address and show up at his door with a plate of cookies. Surely, the little dragon liked cookies, and no doubt, Twinkerbell did, too. It would be Avery's way of apologizing for scaring the crap out of the little dragon.

Then she'd remember the woman with them and all the fantasies she'd been having about Ticked-Off Guy flew out the window. They probably landed somewhere close to the landfill, which is where fantasies about married men belonged.

Avery sighed and sat at the table, all alone, and ate her homemade chili. She'd even baked cornbread with corn in it to go with the chili. While it was no doubt delicious, she barely noticed.

Why couldn't she get Ticked-Off Guy out of her head? Several responses haunted her.

Because she was an idiot?

Because she was simple-minded?

Because she was crazy?

She couldn't even remember the last time she'd witnessed someone that angry, unless you counted the woman at the market the other day whose husband had snarled at her for God knows what. Standing behind them in line, Avery got an earful of a whole new vocabulary.

She finished her lunch and put everything away. There wasn't much of a mess, because she was a clean-as-you-go woman. She headed to her bedroom, but when she got there, she forgot why she'd entered the room.

Her doorbell rang, which never happened, unless it was Halloween, and that was nothing more than a memory now.

Without thinking, she pulled open the door.

There stood Ticked-Off Guy. With his two kids. The little boy, sans dragon costume, clung to his leg, hiding his face against his dad's jeans. The little girl grinned and waved at her. She looked cute in her Twinkerbell costume.

Ticked-Off Guy said, "I decided the best thing to do was bring Jett over so he could see that you weren't planning to eat him."

Avery nodded, wishing she didn't find Ticked-Off Guy so mesmerizing.

He knelt down. In the process, he unattached his kid from his leg. The boy covered his eyes with his little hands. "Jett, say hello to the witch."

"Nooooo!" And then he began to sob.

Avery hated to see anyone cry, especially a toddler who was apparently deathly afraid of her. She went down on her knees and put a hand on his head, trying to comfort him.

Jett screamed bloody murder.

"Jett, that's enough. Say hello."

"Nooooo! Don't make me, Daddy. She wants to eat me in her Cown Flakes."

"I don't eat Corn Flakes," Avery said.

His small shoulders shook like crazy. "In a bowl of ice cweam, then."

"I do have ice cream," she said. "What's your favorite flavor?"

"Stwahbewwy."

"Yum, that's what I have."

"Don't eat me!" he screamed again, then dropped his hands and lunged at her. He was so shocked when he saw her, he skidded to a halt and demanded, "Whewa's the witch?"

"I'm the witch."

"Nooooo!"

"I look different now because I made myself up to look like a witch for Halloween."

He blinked his big green eyes at her, dispensing two more huge tears. "Huh?"

"Would you like to see me make myself into a witch?"

"Nooooo!"

"How about a brownie, then. Do you like brownies?"

"I love bwownies!"

"With nuts?"

"Yessssss!"

Avery stood. "Would you like to come in for milk and brownies?" she asked Ticked-Off Guy.

"I would!" the little girl said, not giving her dad a chance to answer. "I'm Kenzie. What's your name?"

"Avery, but everyone calls me Avery."

Kenzie laughed at the joke and extended her hand, like she was a miniature adult. She looked up at her dad. "Can we stay for milk and brownies, Daddy?"

"Uh, sure." He shook his head, as if trying to equate the witch who'd scared Jett to death with the woman in front of him now. "How'd you make yourself into such a believable witch?"

"I did my research." And then, she smiled at him.

He sucked in a breath.

The kids stepped over the threshold, but Ticked-Off Guy remained frozen on the porch.

After a few seconds, he seemed to regain his senses.

From three feet away, inside the house, the three of them stared at him like he was some kind of grouch or something.

Avery shook her head and extended her hands to the kids. "He's sure to follow, if we head to the kitchen."

Jett and Kenzie giggled.

Avery couldn't help herself. She giggled, too.

She situated the kids at her farmhouse table, then pulled out the milk and poured three glasses before she cut and plated the brownies.

"I'll take milk, too," Ticked-Off Guy said from the kitchen doorway.

Avery turned to look at him and flashed him another smile. "Nice of you to join us."

He didn't smile back. "Jett said you had a green face, pointy teeth, and fingernails so long and red, he thought you were going to use them to cut him up into tiny pieces."

"I wore a black witch's gown and a black pointy hat on my head, too."

Under ordinary circumstances, Clancy might have had second thoughts about messing with a witch.

But, these weren't ordinary circumstances.

His kid had come home crying and screaming and carrying on that the witch was going to eat him. He couldn't let that pass. "You scared the holy crap outta Jett."

Her eyes shot to his son, then back to him. "I'm sorry for that."

Jett nodded, though he was smiling now, not crying.

"You can lose the innocent act. How many other unsuspecting kids did you send home, crying hysterically on Halloween?"

"I—"

"Don't bother trying to justify your actions."

"But I'm not—"

"I have half a mind to report you to the authorities," he yelled, shaking a finger in her face.

Good grief! Had he lost his mind?

That's when Clancy looked at her again, really studying her. He immediately got lost in her big cornflower-blue eyes.

That threw him and he lost his train of thought.

Since when did he register the color of someone's eyes, let alone the witch's, who wanted to eat his kid?

For God's sake, how did he even know they were cornflower-blue?

She smiled at him again, though it looked a bit uncertain to him.

Clancy knew in that moment, he was in for a world of hurt.

Green face, long red nails, and pointed teeth or not, her freaking smile snagged him but good.

Avery poured another glass of milk, then said, "My

oldest brother's a cop at Sweet Creek Sheriff's Office. I'll give you his number, if you want it."

Ticked-Off Guy barked out a laugh, but it wasn't at all amused.

Avery decided she must be losing her touch. Before she could comment further, his daughter spoke up.

"What's your last name?" Kenzie asked. "Ours is O'Rourke. We're mostly Irish."

Avery tore her gaze away from their father and said, "My last name is Lark. I'm mostly Heinz Fifty-seven."

"What's that?" Kenzie asked.

"I'm a little bit of several different nationalities."

"Oh. Is that a problem?"

Avery grinned. "Never has been."

"Need any help?" Ticked-Off Guy asked.

"No, but thanks."

She brought the four glasses of milk to the table first, on a tray, then the plated brownies. After that, she set out napkins for everyone and took her chair.

Ticked-Off Guy eventually slid into the remaining chair. "It smells like chili in here."

"That's what I had for lunch, with cornbread."

He nodded, but continued to stare at her.

"Have I grown a wart on the end of my nose?" she couldn't resist asking.

It took him a moment to respond. "Was I staring?"

"Yes."

"It's not polite to stare, Daddy," Kenzie said.

Avery grinned. Kenzie sounded exactly like her fifth-grade teacher, who'd been so stern, squirrels saluted her when they dashed across the outside windowsills.

Ticked-Off Guy shook his head. "I'm having a hard time equating the picture in my mind of you as the witch Jett described, and the woman serving us brownies and milk."

"The witch was me in costume. This is the real me."

Clancy hesitated, then said, "I prefer the real you better."

"Thanks, I think."

"Daddy, maybe you should have a brownie and stop staring at Avery."

He spared his daughter a glance, and realized the three of them had already taken a brownie. He reached for one of the chocolate squares.

"What's your first name, Mr. O'Rourke?" Avery asked.

"Clancy."

"And what's your wife's name?"

"My wife?"

She nodded. "The woman who brought the kids trick-or-treating?"

"That's not my wife, that's my youngest sister. Her name is Maureen, but we call her Mo."

"Oh."

"We don't gots a mommy," Jett said, reaching for his second brownie.

"You don't?" Avery asked, surprised and a little shocked over his declaration. Then it dawned on her, it was good news that Clancy didn't have a wife…unless, of course, he had a steady girlfriend.

"She left two years ago," Kenzie said. "She didn't want kids or Daddy anymore."

Avery examined Kenzie's tone for sorrow or regrets, but found none. "I'm sorry to hear that."

Kenzie shrugged. "We get along fine without her, don't we, Daddy?"

"Only because Mo babysits you two while I'm at work."

"I love Auntie Mo," Jett said. "Gwammy made me the dwagon costume for Halloween. I'm glad you're not a witch anymowa. I don't like witches, 'specially if they wanna eat me."

"I never eat people," Avery assured him.

"Would you like to come to our house for dinner?" Ticked-Off Guy, AKA Clancy, blurted out.

His kids did a double-take, probably wondering if he'd lost his mind.

"Sure. When?"

"Tonight?"

It was short notice, but Avery didn't have any Sunday-night plans. "That sounds like fun. What can I bring?"

"Bring?"

"You know, food- or beverage-wise?"

"Oh. Nothing. It's Sunday night. We always have spaghetti and meatballs on Sunday night."

"I love spaghetti. What time?"

"Five?"

That was early, considering she'd just had lunch, but maybe they turned in early. "How 'bout if I bring brownies for dessert?"

"Yesssssss!" Jett yelled. "You maked weally good bwownies!"

Not long later, she saw them out the front door. Good-byes were exchanged and she watched as they made their way to the main sidewalk.

They all looked back and waved.

She turned to step back inside, then remembered she didn't know their address. "Hey, where do you live?"

Kenzie shouted out the street number, then ran back up to the porch. "You won't forget, will you?"

"Pinky swear, I won't."

CHAPTER 4

SUNDAY DINNER WITH THE O'ROURKES

Avery arrived with the last of the brownies she'd baked that morning. Well, almost the last. She'd kept two aside for herself. Tomorrow, she'd have to buy another mix, because she loved brownies as much as Jett and Kenzie did.

She knocked on the door to announce her arrival.

Kenzie opened it before Avery had pulled her hand away. The little girl flung herself at Avery, circling her legs in a hug. "I'm so glad you came!"

"Me, too," Jett said, flinging himself at her legs, too.

Avery lost her balance and went backward, landing on her butt.

Jett and Kenzie thought that was funny and Jett climbed on top of her belly and began to bounce.

A moment later, Clancy, still looking like Ticked-Off Guy, scooped him off of her and set him in the entryway. He turned and held out a hand to her.

Avery handed him the plate of brownies instead of her hand.

He transferred the plate to his left hand and again offered her a hand up.

She accepted it and in the next instant, she was on her feet. "Thank you."

"No problem. The kids have been really excited about you coming for dinner."

She smiled. "The sauce smells delicious."

"It's nothing fancy," Clancy warned. "Classico Tomato Basil, spaghetti, meatballs, salad, and warm bread."

"Do you make your own meatballs?"

He nodded. "I make several dozen at once, cook them, and freeze them until I need them."

"That's smart."

He smirked. "I like to spend as little time in the kitchen as possible."

"I take it that means you don't like to cook."

"Exactly. I only do it because I have to."

"Will Maureen be joining us?"

"I asked her, but she had other plans." He led her to the kitchen.

Much to her surprise, it was a cook's delight. "Wow."

"I thought you might like it, considering I assume you *do* like to cook."

"This would certainly be my dream kitchen," she said, poking around, opening cupboards and drawers. When she realized what she was doing was rude, she said, "I'm sorry. I just wondered how everything was laid out."

"Snoop away," Clancy said.

"Daddy, hand over the brownies," Kenzie said, her little voice sounding stern.

Belatedly, Clancy stopped looking at Avery and gave the brownie plate to his daughter.

She set the plate on the counter.

"Would you like a glass of Montepulciano?"

"That sounds nice, but I'll wait for dinner."

The timer on the stove went off.

"Go wash your hands, kids," he said.

The scampered off down the hall.

"The table looks nice."

"Thanks." He glanced that way. "I would've put a tablecloth on, but being that it's spaghetti night, I decided not to."

"Another smart move. What can I do?"

"Slice the bread?"

She smiled at him, which made him suck in his breath again. "I can handle that."

He took the pasta off the stove and drained it in a colander he'd placed in the sink. After that, he poured the pasta into the pot of sauce and stirred it up good before he dumped it into a large bowl.

Avery placed the bread in a basket lined with a napkin. "Where are the meatballs?"

"In the oven. Potholders are in the drawer to the right."

She set the bread on the table, grabbed a potholder, and pulled out the meatballs. "These are huge."

"I eat two and the kids split one. That leaves one for you."

"I'll try to do it justice."

"You have beautiful eyes."

"So do you."

They stared at each other until Jett stepped between them. "Don't fowget the salad, Daddy."

"I won't, son." He placed the spaghetti in the middle of the table and went to the fridge for the salad. "Okay, guys, let's eat."

He poured milk for the kids and wine for himself and Avery, then took his chair. "Who wants to say grace?"

With three sets of eyes pointed at her, Avery said, "I will."

They all joined hands and she said, "Thank you, God, for this delicious food and the O'Rourke family, who is so generously sharing it tonight. Amen."

"That was nice, Avery," Kenzie said. "How are you at slurping 'sketti?"

"I learned 'sketti slurping at a young age," Avery said, her tone serious. "I'm quite good at it."

Clancy rolled his eyes, like he thought she was kidding.

She gave him a look. "You doubt me?"

"Well…."

"Get ready, 'cuz you ain't seen nuthin yet." She proceeded to dish up spaghetti for the two children and herself before she handed the spaghetti fork to Clancy.

Clancy watched his kids and the woman who was supposed to be an adult with astonishment as they had a 'sketti slurping contest.

Kenzie and Jett laughed.

Kenzie said, "You *are* good at it, Avery."

"I wanna be that good," Jett said, shoving more spaghetti into his mouth.

"The trick is to put only a couple of pieces of 'sketti on your fork at once," Avery said. "Otherwise, it all gets jumbled up and hard to slurp."

Jett immediately spit the spaghetti out of his mouth.

To her credit, Avery didn't make a face or gag or scold him. "Want me to show you?"

Jett nodded enthusiastically.

Avery pushed away from the table and walked around to Jett's side of the table. She picked up his fork and twirled it in the pasta, leaving about eight inches dangling. "Open wide."

Jett opened his mouth as wide as he could.

"Now, close your mouth over the spaghetti and start slurping."

He did as she instructed and slurped faster than Clancy

had ever seen him slurp.

"Yay!" Jett yelled after he swallowed it. "You teached me how to sluwp, Avery." He threw his arms around her neck and hugged her, and after that, he high-fived her.

Again, to her credit, she didn't flinch when his hands, which were covered in spaghetti sauce, ended up in her hair and on her blouse. "Wanna try it by yourself?"

Jett nodded. "You might have to help me, though."

"I will, if you need it." She showed him how to hold his fork, then helped him twirl the spaghetti. "There," she said on the second try, "you've got it."

"Thank you, Avery. Did you see that, Daddy. I sluwped as fast as Avery did!"

Clancy smiled at his son. "Amazing, Jett. Congratulations!"

As if she didn't have spaghetti sauce all over her blouse or in her hair, Avery retook her seat and reached for a meatball.

When she looked up at Clancy with those big corn-flower-blue eyes of hers, he took yet another tumble toward falling in love with her.

CHAPTER 5

15 DAYS AFTER HALLOWEEN

Avery walked around the corner to Clancy's street, excited about the prospect of babysitting his kids. It wasn't so much that they were his kids (though she already loved them and their silly antics), but she was excited to see him again. Ticked-Off Guy wasn't really all that bad when you got to know him.

When he'd asked if she could watch his kids, she'd inquired why. "You know Mo makes jewelry?"

"She showed me some of her pieces. She's quite talented."

He nodded. "She has to set up for a show that's happening tomorrow, and she couldn't do it until tonight. That being the case, I need someone to watch Jett and Kenzie."

Things were looking up. No, it wasn't a date, but hells-bells, maybe they could get to know each better when he got home.

Kenzie and Jett were sitting on the front stoop when she made her way up the sidewalk. They screamed and ran to hug her. Truth be told, she liked their hugs. She liked that they liked her. She liked Clancy, too, but she wasn't about to tell him that.

"Where's your dad?" she asked, seeing no sign of him.

"He's getting his suit on," Kenzie said. "He's got a big-deal dinner meeting tonight."

Avery smiled. Kenzie always sounded so grown up when she parroted her dad. "Let's go inside. I brought you guys a surprise."

"You did?" They jumped up-and-down and clapped their hands.

Before they reached the door, it opened and there stood Clancy. Avery almost fell over. What he did for a suit ought to be illegal. It was black, and he wore a white dress shirt and a black-and-red striped tie under the suit coat. He had black shoes on his feet, with red socks.

"Wow, Daddy!" Kenzie said, inspecting him from head to foot.

"You look diff'went," Jett said.

"You look amazing," Avery said, then wished she'd kept her mouth shut.

Clancy aimed a sexy grin at her. "Thanks."

He stepped aside and motioned the three of them inside. A moment later, his gaze went to the street. "There's Louise now."

"Who's Louise?" Avery asked, turning to look.

"My marketing VP. She orchestrated this evening without consulting me, which is another reason why I needed a babysitter."

Avery's excitement at seeing him lost a little of it's fizz. "What time will you be back?"

"I'm not sure, exactly. Do you need to be somewhere else?"

"No, but I'm kind of a time girl."

He nodded. "I'll call if we're going to be later than ten."

She couldn't help looking at her watch. Five-thirty. "Sounds good. Did you want me to fix dinner, or have the kids already eaten?"

"I ordered a pizza. It should be here any minute."

"I told Daddy he should ask what kind you like," Kenzie said, "but he didn't listen to me."

"I'll eat anything but anchovies."

"What awa anchovies?" Jett asked.

"Little salty fishes."

He made a face.

Kenzie sounded disgusted when she added, "Daddy always orders half cheese and half pepperoni."

Avery smiled. "Actually, that sounds delicious."

Louise left her vehicle and came up the walk. "Ready?"

Clancy smiled at her. "Yep." He knelt down to give the kids a hug and a kiss, then straightened. "Mind Avery now, okay?"

They nodded, though it was plainly obvious they didn't want him to go.

"Louise, this is Avery Lark. She lives around the corner. Avery, this is Louise Draper."

Louise smiled warmly and extended her hand. "So nice to meet you, Avery."

She glanced back at Clancy, who said to her, "You look stunning."

She grinned. "Bought a new dress for this occasion."

Avery suddenly felt dowdy in her jeans and sweater.

Clancy made eye contact with her. "You have my number if anything comes up."

A little demon took over her mind for a minute. "I also know how to dial nine-one-one," she threw back at him, which made him frown.

"I hope that's the last number you have to call tonight."

Avery and the two little ones polished off the entire

pizza over the course of two hours. In between times, they played games and sang songs.

At eight-thirty, she got them into their jammies and read them a couple of stories. Jett fell asleep right away, but Kenzie fought off the Sandman.

Avery carried Jett down the hall from Kenzie's room to his bed, surprised by how heavy he was for a little guy.

"Avery?"

She turned to look at Kenzie, who stood in Jett's doorway. "I'll be right with you, sweetie."

"I know, but I wanted to tell you how much I like you."

Avery crossed Jett's room, leaving the door open so she could hear him if he woke up. She squatted down so she was more at Kenzie's height. "I like you, too, Kenzie."

The little girl smiled at her. "Do you have a boy-friend?"

"No."

"I do. His name is Brennan and he's in first grade."

"Ah. An older man, huh?"

Kenzie's smile widened into a grin. "I never told Dad-dy about him."

"Why not?"

"Daddy told me once I'm too young to have a boy-friend."

"Five is a little young, I suppose."

"The thing is, Brennan doesn't know I like him, so maybe he doesn't count as a boyfriend."

"You know, I think you may be right." She took Kenzie's hand and led her back to her bedroom, where she tucked her in. "Sweet dreams, honey."

"Thank you, Avery. That's a really nice thing to say."

Five minutes later, Avery was back in the family room, straightening up. She put the games away and tossed away the paper plates they'd eaten their pizza and brownies on.

After that, she dug the two small, forgotten packages out of her purse and set them on the breakfast bar. They were labeled JETT and KENZIE.

She glanced at her watch, surprised to find it was ten-fifteen. Maybe Clancy was on his way home, or maybe he'd gone home with Louise for a little somethin'-somethin' to keep him going.

Avery kicked off her shoes and laid down on the sofa. It was fun being with the kids, but she'd had a long, tiring day. She closed her eyes and the next thing she knew, it was morning. She jerked up off the sofa and glanced at her watch. Seven-twenty. Where the heck was Clancy?

She bolted down the hall to the master bedroom, but he wasn't there and his bed hadn't been slept in. Avery didn't know whether to be angry or worried. She heard the front door open and ran back down the hall, but it was Mo, not Clancy.

"I wondered if you'd spend the night," Mo said, her tone coy.

"I did, but only because Clancy never came home."

Mo's eyes widened. "He didn't? Are the kids still asleep?"

Avery nodded. "He was supposed to call at ten if he was going to be late, but he didn't do that, either."

Mo frowned. "That's not like Clancy at all. Have you tried calling him?"

"No. I fell asleep on the sofa and just woke up. I went to see if he was in his bedroom, but he's not."

Mo pulled out her phone and called her brother. "Where the heck are you?" she demanded. "What? … Is Louise okay? … You should've at least called, you big lug nut! … I don't know, I'll ask her." She held the phone away from her ear and looked at Avery. "Can you stay until noon?"

"I suppose so, but…will you take Kenzie to school?"

"I don't need to be at my jewelry show until eight-thirty. I can drop her off on my way." She started to put the phone back to her ear, but Avery held up her hand.

"Ask him if it's okay to take Jett home with me? I have some work to finish that's time sensitive."

Finally, she put the phone back to her ear. "Can Avery take Jett home with her? … Okay." She nodded at Avery.

Avery nodded back. She wanted to know in the worst way if he was all right, but she put a damper on the thought. They didn't have that kind of relationship.

Several minutes later, Mo hung up. "This is terrible."

"What happened?"

"Louise's husband had a heart attack last night. He nearly died."

That didn't explain why Clancy hadn't called.

"Clancy said he and his phone got separated until a few minutes ago. He used it to call the ambulance and then he set it down and Louise thought it was Carl's, because they look alike, and she picked it up. When he got his phone back, Clancy didn't have your number, so he couldn't call you."

As convoluted excuses went, his was mostly viable.

"I'd better wake the kids up," Mo said. "Would you mind getting the cereal and the other stuff out? We're going to be pushed for time."

"Sure." Avery tracked down the cereal boxes, bowls, and spoons, thinking about what she could take along to her house to entertain Jett while she worked.

"Can we open our presents now?" Kenzie asked.

"Sure." She handed them the bags with their names on them.

Kenzie had hers opened first. She pulled out the jewelry box and opened it. "It's a Twinkerbell necklace. I love it, Avery! Can I wear it now?"

"Of course."

Kenzie handed her the box and Avery unhooked the necklace. A moment later, it was hanging around the little girl's neck.

"Thank you!" She danced around the kitchen, then stopped in front of her aunt. "Look, Auntie Mo."

"It's beautiful," Mo said.

Jett had a jewelry box in his bag, too. He opened it and screamed, "Yaaaaay!"

"What is it?" Mo asked.

"I watch with Elmo on in. Thank you, Avery!" He threw himself at Avery's knees and hugged them. "Can I wear it now?"

"Absolutely."

"Will you teach me how to tell time?"

"We'll work on it," Avery said. "It's a process."

"What's a process?" he asked.

"It's like reading a book," Mo intervened. "It takes time."

Grateful Mo had answered the question, Avery cleaned up quickly after the kids ate, then Mo and Kenzie were on their way. She found a large handle bag in the laundry room and let Jett pick out a few things to take with him. He chose three Fisher-Price toys, two games, and what was left of the brownies.

She carried the bag while he skipped along in front of her. "I never goed to your house by myself a'fowa."

"I know. I hope Twinkle didn't mind being outside all night."

"Who's Twinkle."

"My dog."

Jett stared at her with owl eyes. "You neva told me you have a dog."

"Now you know."

"Whewa was he when we came to yowa house a'fowa?"

"In the back yard. He likes to be outside."

"Does he gots a ball?"

"He sure does."

"Can I thwow it fowa him?"

"Sure."

"Will you put yowa witch clothes on?"

"Really?"

"Yeah, but not the gween face owa the pointy teeth owa the long wed fingas."

"Are you sure? I mean, you won't freak out will you?"

"I pwomise I won't!"

Avery considered the little guy for a few seconds. "What shall we do first, let Twinkle in the house or get my witch clothes on?"

"If you let Twinkle in, I can play with him while you put yowa witch clothes on."

Out of the mouth of babes. "I need to feed him and give him fresh water first. He's probably hungry and thirsty."

"Okay."

Inside the house, Jett trotted along beside her as she headed for the laundry room.

"That's a big dish."

"He has a big appetite."

Avery also filled Twinkle's water dish, then opened the laundry room door. The golden retriever was on the stoop and came roaring in, happy to see her. He also liked the little person standing beside her.

Jett giggled. "He likes me!"

"He sure does."

It had never occurred to Avery that her dog might like to have kids around to play with.

CHAPTER 6

NOVEMBER 16, THE AFTERNOON

Avery was exhausted, but it was a comfortable kind of exhaustion. She absolutely adored Jett, who followed her and Twinkle into her home office. She finished her work on the computer, then the three of them took a walk along Sugar Plum Creek. Twinkle splashed in the water, but she and Jett decided it was too chilly to stick a toe in.

Back at the house, they had peanut butter and jelly sandwiches for lunch, brownies for dessert, and afterward, they laid down for a nap. Jett snuggled up to her like she was his mom, or something.

"I love you, Avery."

"I love you, too, Jett."

When they woke up, Jett begged her to put her witch costume on. Avery had planned to bake more brownies. Her first thought was, if she was careful, wearing her witch costume would probably work out okay. Her second thought was, she'd better secure the sleeves with rubberbands, or she'd be dragging them in batter mix.

"Are you gonna be my helper?"

"Maybe, but I'd watha play with Twink."

She grinned at his abbreviation of her dog's name. "All right, but stay in the kitchen, so I know what you're both doing."

He nodded, his expression serious. "Whewa's Twink's ball?"

"In the laundry room, in his toy box."

Jett tore off to find it. When he came back, Avery already had the witch costume on. "Yowa pwetty without a gween face."

She smiled at him. "Thanks."

Jett sat on the floor and began to throw the ball for Twinkle. "What kinda dog is Twink?"

"A golden retriever." She grabbed two rubberbands from a drawer, secured her sleeves, then opened the box of brownie mix and dumped it into a mixing bowl.

"Is Twink a boy or a giwa?"

"A boy."

"Will you let me come back and play with him?"

"Sure. Anytime."

"Can Auntie Mo come, too? And Kenzie?"

"You bet." She cracked two eggs, added the oil and water, and stirred, then dumped in the chopped walnuts.

The doorbell rang.

Jett looked up, but all he said was, "Someone's at the doowa."

"I heard. I'll be right back."

He nodded and rolled the ball for Twink again.

Usually, Avery checked to see who it was through the peephole, but today, she forgot. She also forgot to leave the wooden spoon in the kitchen. She pulled the door open, not surprised to find Clancy on her porch, though he was hours past when he said he'd pick Jett up.

"Is that your magic wand?" Clancy asked, amused.

"I'm making brownies."

His amusement faded as his eyes wandered over her. "Why are you wearing your witch costume?"

"Jett asked me to."

He scowled. "Please tell me you didn't eat my son."

Little footsteps came running across the living room. "Hi, Daddy!"

In what must have been their time-honored greeting, Jett leaped toward his father and Clancy caught him, swinging him in the air before he hugged him. "How's my little guy today?"

"Avery has a dog, Daddy. His name is Twinkle!"

He glanced at Avery, again taking in her outfit from the tip of her witch hat to the bottom of her hem, then back up again, until his eyes landed on the rubberbands. "Does she." Not a question, but a statement.

Avery waved her wooden spoon like it *was* Twinkerbell's magic wand. "I need to put the brownies in the oven." She turned and headed back to the kitchen.

Clancy closed and locked the front door and followed. "What did you two do today?" he asked Jett.

"We taked Twink for a walk down by the cweek."

"I bet that was fun."

"It was. When we comed back, Avery fixed PB-and-J sammies, and she let me have banana slices on mine."

"That was nice of her."

Jett wriggled in his dad's arms. "Put me down, Daddy. Twink wants to catch mowa balls."

Clancy set his son down and watched as he rushed over to hug Twink.

Avery stood in front of the oven, ogling Clancy. When he started to turn toward her, she dragged her gaze away and returned the pot holder to the drawer.

"Thanks for watching Jett."

"It's not a problem. We've been having fun, haven't we, Jett."

"We have! Don't you like Avery in hewa witch clothes, Daddy? She's so pwetty without a gween face and pointy teeth and long wed fingas."

Clancy nodded. "She sure is."

Avery set the timer and turned away to clean up the brownie-making mess. Her face felt so hot, she thought she might explode. "You've had an exciting twenty-four hours."

"I don't know that I'd call it exciting," Clancy said, coming up to stand close to her. "Carl keeled over during dinner, and the next thing I knew, it was this morning. I ran home to have a shower and change clothes before I headed back to the hospital, then to work." He folded his nicely muscled arms over his chest. "It was weird being at home with no one else there."

"I was hewa, Daddy. Did you know Avery makes 'puta games?"

"No, I didn't." He looked back at Avery. "There's a lot about you I don't know."

"I'm boring," she blurted out for lack of anything better to say.

"I seriously doubt that," Clancy said. His eyes dropped to her lips. "How can I repay you for bailing me out?"

"I don't need money for watching Jett, if that's what you're asking."

"I was thinking of something a little more personal, like a kiss."

The brim of her witch hat took that opportunity to flop down in front of her eyes, which was a good thing. While his suggestion tantalized and intrigued her, it also scared the hell out of her. She leaned her head back. "A kiss?"

He reached out and plucked the hat off her head. "Yeah, you know. My lips touch your lips…."

Her breath came faster. Her insides clenched with excitement. Her girl parts got all fluttery. "I suppose that would be okay."

He smirked at her. "Just okay? I was hoping you'd jump up and down with anticipation."

"Not likely," she lied.

His smirk settled into a satisfied grin. He leaned closer and whispered, "May this be the first of many."

Little hands tugged on his pant leg. "Daddy, why ah you kissing Avery?"

Clancy pulled away from a kiss he never wanted to end. "Because."

"Because isn't an ansa," said his little parrot.

Clancy expanded his answer for his son's benefit. "Because I wanted to thank her for taking care of you."

"She loves me and I love hewa back, so why wouldn't she take cawa me?"

Staring into Avery's cornflower-blue eyes, Clancy almost got lost, but then Jett tugged on his pant leg again. "Daddy?"

He dragged his eyes away from Avery's and looked down at his son. "You're easy to love, Jett."

"I am?" He smiled.

"You sure are." He squatted down so he could meet his son's gaze. "Get your stuff together. We need to go pick up Kenzie, then how about going to Pizza King for dinner?"

Jett's eyes filled with tears. "I'd watha stay here. Avery's making bwownies and I love bwownies."

Avery intervened. "Leave Jett here while you go pick up Kenzie. The brownies should be done by the time you get back. I'll send some home with you and you can have them for dessert."

"Yaaaaay!" Jett screamed.

"I have a better idea," Clancy said. "Why don't you come with us? Afterward, we can stop by the jewelry show and see how Mo's doing."

The woman with cornflower-blue eyes gave him a slow blink, as if stunned that he'd invited her along. "That sounds…like fun." And then she licked her lips.

Man, could he think of some things that beautiful mouth of hers could do….

Later, at Pizza King, they selected a table close to the kids' playroom, where he could keep an eye on Jett and Kenzie. "What kind of pizza do you like?"

"A combo, as long as it doesn't have anchovies or onions on it."

"Thank God you didn't say pepperoni."

"I actually like pepperoni, but I like a combo better, with tomatoes on it after it's cooked."

"That sounds good." He hesitated, then said, "Would you like to take in a movie this weekend?"

"A movie?" she asked with wide eyes, then stupidly clarified. "I usually watch movies at home."

"What about dinner, then? We could go to your place and watch a movie after?"

"Which night?" she asked, as if she had weekend plans.

"Either is fine by me. My folks are taking the kids for the weekend."

That sounded promising, except that Avery, who had the major hots for Clancy, wasn't the kind of woman who jumped into bed just like that—especially not with a man she'd only known for two weeks.

That begged the question, was he inviting her to have sex with him, or was it really a dinner-and-a-movie night? She decided to test the waters. "I could fix dinner."

"Let's save that for another night."

Avery nodded. No sex, then, just dinner-and-a-movie, and apparently a second date sometime down the road. Would there also be a third? And a fourth? God, she hoped so!

He stood. "I'll go order. What would you like to drink?"

"A beer?"

"Any preference?"

"Something not too hoppy or grapefruity."

He nodded and headed to the counter.

Avery fanned herself.

Did Clancy O'Rourke have any idea what he was doing to her?

CHAPTER 7

NOVEMBER 16, BEDTIME

Avery informed Clancy on the way home that he could drop her at his house. She needed some fresh air, and she could walk the short distance home, especially after eating three slices of pizza.

All the way to the corner, she kept reminding herself that she didn't jump into bed with a man she'd just met. In fact, she didn't jump into bed with any man. If and when she had sex with Clancy, it would be her first time, which was kind of pathetic, when she thought about it. After all, how many twenty-nine-year-old virgins were there running around Sweet Creek, Colorado?

From his house to her house, she kept reminding herself that she'd never been attracted to a man before, at least not like she was to Clancy. It wasn't like she'd never met any other eligible bachelors, either, but none of them had affected her like Clancy.

Once she got inside her house, she went directly to the back door to let Twinkle in. After that, she headed to her bedroom. It was almost nine o'clock, which was early for her, but she was tired. Babysitting Jett had taken a lot of energy, and after they ate, they'd spent ninety minutes wandering around the jewelry show. Finally, Jett had asked Clancy to carry him, and he'd fallen asleep on his dad's shoulder.

Avery had never been so envious of anyone, as she was of Jett in that moment.

As she climbed into her PJs, she wondered how it would be, to be a part of a family like Clancy's. To have children with him. To live and love with him for the rest of her life. To see their grandchildren grow up to be adults. To....

The doorbell rang, cutting off her thoughts and startling her. Who the heck would come calling at this hour?

She headed to the front door peered through the peephole. Clancy!

The doorbell rang again.

She almost didn't answer, but her hand wasn't taking orders from her brain. She opened the door. "What're you doing here, and who's watching the kids?"

"I came to kiss you goodnight, and Mo is watching the kids."

"She didn't say she was headed to your house when we saw her at the jewelry show."

Clancy smirked at her. "She read the signs."

"Signs? What signs?"

"The ones sparking between you and me." He stepped over the threshold.

Avery backed up a step.

He moved closer.

She took two more steps back.

"Don't run, Avery."

"I'm not."

"Like hell." He reached for her and lowered his head. And then he kissed her.

Somehow, Avery's arms ended up wrapped around his neck.

He picked her up, kicked the door shut, then turned to lock it. "Which way to your bedroom?" he whispered against her lips.

"Down the hall…." She dragged his head down for another kiss, then she realized he really was carrying her down the hall. She pulled her head away and said, "Stop right here!"

"Why?"

"Because."

"Because why?"

"Because I'm not putting out for you."

He frowned. "Did I misread you?"

Avery was so hot for him, she barely managed the one word that left her mouth. "Misread?"

He nodded and set her back on her feet. "I thought…." He shook his head. "Never mind."

"Never mind what?" She liked being close to him, liked feeling his erection pressing against her, but she wasn't ready to take a tumble in the sheets with him.

He blinked at her, and grimaced.

Avery guessed he was embarrassed because he'd assumed something he shouldn't have assumed. She almost told him it was okay. She'd have as many babies with him as he wanted.

Then reality set in.

She wasn't ready to face the consequences if she ended up pregnant and a baby popped out next July, so why would she offer to have as many babies as he wanted?

Aside from that, she wasn't ready to make love with Clancy O'Rourke, even if he was raring to go.

She considered the accompanying issues as they'd popped into her head.

She loved Kenzie and Jett, so mothering them wouldn't be a problem. And if Clancy gave her a baby, she'd love it, too.

As for making love with him, there was nothing she

wanted more, but shouldn't they have a little making-out time beforehand?

Before her brain could stop her mouth, she said, "We hardly know each other, Clancy. Shouldn't we get better acquainted before we, you know, hit the bedroom?"

It was obvious, he was struggling with her rejection. "Can I at least kiss you?"

Of course! Why was he even asking? "That would be nice."

He wasted no time capturing her mouth, and then he laid the best kiss on her she'd ever experienced.

Yeah, she'd had the birds-and-bees talk when she turned thirteen, but for some reason, boys had never asked her out much, and kissing her was as far as it went with any of them. Much to her chagrin, not one of them had ever tried to cop a feel. It had belatedly occurred to her that her brothers might have threatened any guys who *had* asked her out. If that was true, no wonder she was still a virgin!

The kiss went on forever. Finally, she pulled away. "Doesn't Mo have to go home?"

"She agreed to spend the night, if I didn't come home."

Avery wasn't sure how she felt about that, but she knew one thing for certain. She didn't want Clancy's sister thinking she was an easy lay.

After Clancy left, Avery crawled into bed and thought about things.

She liked Clancy, and he obviously liked her. Certainly, they were compatible in the kissing department, but would they be compatible in the love-making department? How did two people even know that, anyway?

She definitely wanted to find out at some point, but

was it feasible when he had two little kids at home?

An hour later, she decided it was not only feasible, but possible, if and when she decided she was ready to give it a go. She could have a sleepover at his house, or he could bring the kids and have a sleepover at her house. The spare room only needed twin beds, and they'd be set.

She jumped out of bed, because she'd forgotten to brush her teeth, and headed to the bathroom. She studied her reflection in the mirror, wondering why her face was so flushed.

It took her less than a minute to figure it out, and his name was Clancy.

Yep, a sleepover would be just the thing sometime down the road.

CHAPTER 8

THE SUNDAY BEFORE THANKSGIVING

Avery studied the pecan pie and pumpkin roll recipes. Both would be her contributions to Thanksgiving dinner. Try as she might, though, she couldn't concentrate on baking long enough to make a shopping list.

Five days had passed since Clancy had come over to kiss her goodnight. Five days!

She hadn't talked to him once since then.

As if Kenzie had waved her magic wand over her phone, it rang.

"Hi," Clancy said, his deep voice flowing over her like warm honey. "Can you join me and the kids for Thanksgiving dinner?"

Slightly miffed at him without really knowing why, she said, "I wish I could, but my folks are expecting me." Then it dawned on her what he'd said. "Is it just you and the kids?"

"Yeah, I have to work on Wednesday, and on Friday, I'm expecting a conference call I can't miss. My family typically goes up to our mountain cabin for Turkey Day." When she didn't say anything, he added, "They like to make a five-day vacation out of it."

"I see."

He hesitated, then asked, "Is something wrong,?"

A lot was wrong, but maybe they could talk it out if he came to her folks' house for Thanksgiving. "Would you and the kids like to join my family for Thanksgiving?"

His hesitation spoke volumes. "Are you sure it's okay with your folks?"

"Positive. Mom always fixes too much food, anyway."

He remained quiet for a moment. "I'd feel more comfortable if you checked with her first."

"Okay. I'll call you back."

"Better yet, why don't you come over for spaghetti and meatballs tonight?"

Avery wanted to, she really did. She'd even bought six more brownie mixes, and she still had time to bake a batch. "That sounds delicious."

"It will be," he said.

She thought she read an unspoken promise in his voice. "Clancy?"

"Yeah?"

"Are you intent on using me only for your own self-gratification?"

"No, but—"

"Are you sure?"

"Yes, but—"

"Then—"

"Hold on a minute. Hey you guys, did you feed Sushi today? … Okay, then better go take care of it."

"Who's Sushi?"

"Our black goldfish. They forget to feed him without a reminder. Now, back to us."

"Is there really an us?"

"I hope so. You know, Louise's husband is still in the hospital, and that means Louise is also still at the hospital."

"I'm sorry to hear that."

"Me, too, but Carl's doing a lot better. Still, I'm basically running things by myself at work."

Avery didn't know why she'd spaced Carl's heart attack. "When will he be released?"

"Tomorrow, but he's supposed to take it easy for a while."

"I take it that means Louise won't be back to work any time soon."

"That's right." He hesitated, then admitted, "I'm having a problem, Avery."

"What kind of problem?"

"All I can think about is you."

Avery sighed. All she could think about was Clancy, but she wasn't going to admit it to him.

"Are you still there?"

"Yes. Shall I bring brownies?"

He laughed softly. "The kids will like that."

"Should I come at five again?"

"That would be perfect. See you then."

Avery hung up, trying to tamp down the excitement coursing through her body. She picked up her phone again and called her mom. "Is it okay if Clancy and his two kids join us for Thanksgiving?"

"Perfect!" Rachel Lark said. "Your dad and I have been anxious to meet the man you're so hung up on."

"What makes you think I'm hung up on him?" Avery asked.

"Honey, you're our daughter. We can read you like a book. Are you still bringing a pecan pie and the pumpkin roll?"

"Yes. I'm working on my shopping list now."

"Yum. See all of you at one on Thursday. Don't be late.

"We won't."

"Wait!"

"What?"

"Tell me their names."

"Clancy O'Rourke. Kenzie is five and Jett is three. You're gonna love all of them."

"Honey, if you do, I know we will."

Avery finished making her grocery list and hit the market. When she got home, she put everything away, then paced her house, trying to decide if she should call and let Clancy know she couldn't make it for spaghetti and meatballs, after all.

She still hadn't made up her mind by three, so she took Twinkle for a walk down to Sugar Plum Creek. As he was prone to do, he jumped in the water, frolicked for a few minutes, then leaped out onto the bank and shook himself. He managed to target Avery pretty well, which she never noticed, so intent were her thoughts on Clancy and whether or not to call and say she couldn't make dinner.

Well, that was stupid. His 'sketti and meatballs were delicious. The real problem was, did he have an extra-curricular activity planned for afterward?

Dinner it was, but she needed to change into something a little sexier, but not too sexy.

At five 'til five, she left her house and walked around the block to Clancy's.

Kenzie and Jett sat on the stoop once more, waiting for her. They jumped up and made a run for her, but this time, she was prepared and managed to stay on her feet.

"We missed you," Kenzie said, hugging her knees extra tight.

"We did," Jett agreed, also holding her knees extra tight.

"I missed both of you, too."

"Did you bwing bwownies?" Jett asked, trying to see what was on the plate.

"I did. Want to see?" She lowered the plate and let him examine the chocolaty squares.

"We gots ice cweam to put on top," he informed her, grinning.

"We like ice cream on our brownies," Kenzie said. "Do you?"

"I've never had ice cream on a brownie before."

"You haven't?" they cried in unison.

"Never."

"That's sad," Kenzie said.

"Weally sad," Jett agreed.

"I've always liked my brownies just they way they are, but ice cream on top sounds yummy, too."

Mo opened the front door. "Hi, Avery."

"Hi, Mo. Are you staying for dinner?"

"I was going to, but Mom called and wants my help doing something Thanksgiving-related, so I'm headed that way, instead. She promised to feed me, but unfortunately, it won't be 'sketti and meatballs." She bent over to give her niece and nephew a kiss and a hug. "You guys have fun, okay?"

The kids nodded and turned to run into the house with the brownies. They had to squeeze past their dad to get in.

Clancy stood in the doorway looking manly, and hungry.

Avery's heart somersaulted and her body began to tingle. Was he hungry for her? "Hi."

"Hi." He smiled and his eyes did an appreciative perusal down her body and back up. "You look nice."

"So do you," she said, glad she'd changed out of her jeans and into slacks and a lightweight, scoop-neck sweater. She took the three steps up. "The kids have the brownies."

"I noticed." Clancy leaned down and kissed her. And kissed her. Then Jett started tugging on his pant leg. "How come yowa kissing Avery, Daddy?"

Clancy grinned down at his son. "Because it's really nice."

"How nice?"

"Someday, you'll find out. I thought you two were taking the brownies to the kitchen."

"We ah." Jett turned away and almost made it to the kitchen, except he turned back to look at the two of them, kissing again, and tripped.

Fortunately, Avery had wrapped the plate of brownies with plastic wrap.

Jett landed on his tummy, then rolled over and watched as his dad continued to kiss Avery.

Kenzie joined him on the floor.

Together, they made a decision to have a brownie while they watched.

CHAPTER 9

'SKETTI-SLURPING SUNDAY

Spaghetti slurping aside, Avery's body pulsed with excitement when Kenzie and Jett finally fell asleep and Clancy extended his hand to her. "They're out for the night," he assured her.

It wasn't that she didn't believe him, but did they ever wake up wanting a glass of water, or needing to use the bathroom?

"I wore them out today, Avery. They were practically asleep before their heads hit their pillows." He tugged her closer and slid his arms around her. "Should we get to know each other better on the sofa or in my bedroom?"

"Definitely, on the sofa."

"That's what I figured you'd say." He leaned down and kissed her, then took her hand and led her to the sofa.

Avery kept pace beside him, wishing she wasn't so skittish.

He leaned over to turn out the lamp on the end table, leaving several candles burning on the mantle. They set the mood perfectly.

The problem was, Avery didn't think it was time for a perfect mood. "It's a little dark in here."

"I can light more candles."

"Would you?"

He smiled at her. "You're a hard sell."

Avery didn't have a proper response to that, so she kept quiet.

Clancy got up and lit two more candles, or rather, he switched on two more battery-powered candles before he sat down next to her on the sofa again.

"There's something you should know about me." Avery folded her arms over her middle and looked away, then back at him.

"Okay."

"I've never had intercourse before."

From his expression, he hadn't been expecting that. "You haven't?"

"You sound surprised. Did you think I had?"

"To tell you the truth, I assumed that these days, everyone has had sex by the time they're your age."

"How old do you think I am?"

"Somewhere close to thirty."

"I'm twenty-nine."

His slow smile warmed her. He reached out and pulled her closer. "I like that I'll be your first."

"Is it weird of me to say that I hope you'll be my only?"

"Not at all." He slid his arm over her shoulder. "Can we get back to kissing?"

She nodded.

"God, I love the way you smell, Avery. I love the way you kiss, too." He gave his head a slight shake. "I love everything about you."

Avery had no idea if he was bullshitting her, or if he meant what he said.

In the aftermath of yet another mind-blowing kiss, she decided to go with door number two, certain that a man would only utter the words Clancy had if he really cared about her.

And then she prayed she was right.

Avery spent the next three days mooning over Clancy and his kisses.

Monday had passed with no word from him. Then Tuesday. And Wednesday, until eight o'clock in the evening. Her cell phone rang and it was Clancy.

She prayed fervently that he wasn't calling to cancel coming to dinner at her parents' house.

She let the phone ring five times. "Hello."

"Hi, it's me."

"Me, who?" she asked, trying to sound confused.

"Clancy," he said, his tone amused.

"Ah."

"Did you get your desserts made?"

"I did, and they're going to be delicious."

"Like you."

Avery was torn. Did she respond in-kind, or ask why he was calling?

Before she could decide, he asked, "Why do you always go silent when I compliment you?"

"Honestly, I have no idea."

"Are you vacillating about our relationship?"

"I didn't know we had a relationship." When he didn't say anything, she continued. "I thought relationships involved dates, in addition to kissing."

"We never did get to have that movie night, did we?"

"No."

He blew out a long sigh. "I can't stop thinking about you."

She decided to be honest, as well. "I can't stop thinking about you, either."

"Will you marry me, Avery?"

She laughed, thinking he was teasing. "Two nights of kissing, then a wedding proposal? That's pretty fast, isn't it?"

"When you have the magic we have, it almost seems too slow."

"Magic?"

"Can't you feel it?"

She felt it, all right, but did that mean they were meant to be together forever? "I feel a lot of things when I'm with you."

He sounded relieved when he said, "Good. What time shall I pick you up tomorrow?"

She had expected him to meet her at the folks' house, but the fact that he was picking her up made her think he might have other plans for after dinner that included her. "Is this our first real date?"

"I guess it is. What time?"

"Quarter to one?"

"Sounds good." He hesitated, then asked, "Are you ready to pack an overnight bag? I'd really like to wake up with you in my bed Friday morning."

"Don't you have a conference call on Friday?"

"Yes, but that doesn't mean I can't make love to you."

"Were you serious when you asked me to marry you?"

"Absolutely."

They'd never talked about the kids' mom. Whether she should broach the subject or not, she took the plunge. "What happened with your wife?"

"She didn't want the kids or me anymore. She also wanted sex a little more exciting and I wasn't into sharing or three-ways."

Avery digested that. "She must have been an idiot."

"Why do you say that?"

"I certainly wouldn't want to share you or have three-ways."

"Thank God for that." He hesitated, then asked, "Are you ready to let me make love to you?"

"I've been waiting my entire life for you, Clancy, but I'm not quite ready."

"Do you love me?"

"Yes."

"But not enough to marry me."

"We've only known each other since Halloween."

"That's longer than my folks knew each other before they tied the knot."

"When am I going to meet them?"

"Is that why you're holding back?"

"No, but the responsible thing to do before you get married is to meet your lover's family, isn't it?"

"I suppose you have a point. If they were going to be in town, I'd invite them for spaghetti and meatballs Sunday night."

"Do you have enough meatballs?"

He laughed. "You can come over on Saturday and help me make more."

"There's one problem with that."

"What?"

"I promised Kenzie and Jett that they could come play with Twinkle on Saturday."

"When did you see them?"

"Mo brought them over after school yesterday. We had brownies and milk."

"They never mentioned it. Of course, they were in bed by the time I got home."

"How's Louise's husband?"

"He's doing well. Louise is trying to work from home, but in addition to being our VP of Marketing, she also keeps our computer system going, and right now, it's having problems."

"I can help you out with that."

"You can? How?"

"I'm a techy guru, Clancy."

"You are?"

"As Jett told you, I write game apps, but I also create websites, and I know my way around computer issues."

He sighed. "I suppose that means you'll be bringing your laptop instead of your overnight bag."

"Gosh, you're good-looking and a detective, too," she quipped. "There's one thing, though."

"What's that?"

"You have to promise not to keep kissing me while I work on your IT problem."

"How am I supposed to avoid kissing you, when your kisses drive me wild?"

"They do?"

"Why do you think I asked you to marry me?"

The proper answer would have been, *Because you love me?* Instead, she said, "I'm looking forward to seeing you tomorrow."

He was silent for so long, she thought he wasn't going to respond. Then he said, "I love you, Avery. That's why I asked you to marry me." He hung up without another word.

CHAPTER 10

THANKSGIVING DAY

Avery's parents greeted them at the front door with hugs and kisses. Behind them were Avery's brothers, Drake and Bent, and her sister, Evie.

Doug and Rachel Lark had a history of lamenting that all their offspring were still single. That was probably why they eyed Clancy with interested, speculative gazes. To their credit, however, they resisted uttering more than a welcome. The inquisition, Avery knew, might well come at the dinner table.

Clancy had dressed the kids in adorable Thanksgiving clothes. His mother, who they called Grammy (or Gwammy), had made their outfits. Jett's shirt and Kenzie's pinafore both had the same cartoon turkeys and pumpkins decorating the fabric. Jett wore brown corduroy pants with his shirt and Kenzie had on a brown corduroy pinafore. They looked adorable and her family immediately fell in love with them.

Her parents herded everyone into the kitchen for appetizers, oohing-and-aahing over Avery's desserts.

Clancy had brought along a six-pack of beer and two

bottles of wine, which enamored him to the Larks.

Rachel smiled at the little ones. "I bought sparkling cherry cider for you two. How does that sound?"

"Really good," Kenzie said.

Jett nodded his agreement and asked, "Do we gets bwownies, too?"

"Thanksgiving is a special day, Jett. We have different desserts after dinner, but I promise, next time you come see us, we'll definitely have brownies."

Jett jumped up-and-down and yelled, "Yaaaaay!"

Dinner a short time later was delicious. Rachel never deviated from a traditional Thanksgiving meal of turkey, stuffing, mashed potatoes, gravy, yam casserole with marshmallows on top, cranberry salad, fresh cranberry sauce, and homemade rolls. In addition to the pumpkin roll and pecan pie, her sister had brought a pumpkin pie with a can of whipped cream. Bent supplied a package of mallow pumpkins and a six-pack. Drake also had a package of mallow pumpkins, along with a bottle of *limon-cello*.

After Doug said the blessing, he served turkey on the stack of plates in front of him and passed them around.

Jett stood up on his chair and eyed the offerings. "I want the mawshmallows, please."

Next to him, Clancy shook his head. "My son has a sweet tooth."

"He's going to fit right in with this family," Drake said. "We've all got sweet tooths."

Bent agreed with a nod.

Evie said, "Not me."

Her brothers gaped at her in stunned surprise.

Drake said, "You've got the biggest sweet tooth ever."

"How big?" Jett asked.

"Really, really big," Bent confirmed.

Still standing on his chair, Jett glanced at Evie, his eyes wide. "Can I see it?"

Evie obligingly opened her mouth.

Jett frowned. "I don't see one that's biggew."

"That's because my brothers were teasing me, Jett."

The three-year-old thought about that for a second, then grinned and plopped back down on his knees.

Rachel set Jett's plate on the table. There was a tiny mound of stuffing, a tablespoon of mashed potatoes, and the turkey, all with gravy, and a spoonful of cranberry salad. The other side was covered with mostly marshmallows and a few yams.

As the others filled their plates, Clancy asked Jett, "Are you going to eat all that?"

Jett nodded with anticipation and picked up his spoon.

"Save room for dessert," Kenzie advised. "Your sweet tooth is going to love everything."

Jett grinned and shoved a spoonful of marshmallows into his mouth.

Then the anticipated interrogation began.

Rachel passed the gravy boat. "Clancy, Avery says you met because Jett thought she was going to eat him for Halloween."

The family had a moment of complete silence, then howled with laughter.

"God, I wish I'd been there to see that," Bent said, grinning. "Were you scared, Jett?"

Jett nodded with a frown. "She was weally scawy."

"How scary?" Drake asked, amused.

"Weally, weally, *weally* scawy," Jett said and took another mouthful of marshmallows and an itsy-bitsy piece of yam. "She had a gween face and pointy teeth and long, wed fingas."

"That does sound scary." Rachel glanced at Avery, amused. If her mother had felt sorry for Jett, that glance would've registered disapproval, not amusement. "Avery texted us a picture of herself dressed as a witch. I thought she looked really, really, *really* scary, too."

"FYI, Mom, I bought three ginormous bags of candy and there were only two Baby Ruths left at eight o'clock when I turned out the lights."

"I supposed you polished them off," Doug said.

"Of course," Avery said, grinning. "I can't believe how many kids came knocking on my door." She looked at Clancy, then at Jett. "None of them thought I was going to eat them except Jett."

"Avery babysitted me and dwessed in her witch costume while I played with Twink," Jett said, reaching for his sparkling cider. "She pwomised not to put the gween stuff on hewa face" — he flashed his cute little smile — "ow do the wed fingas or pointy teeth."

"Thank goodness she didn't eat you," Evie said, reaching for a roll. "You might have given her indigestion."

That cracked up everyone at the table except Jett. He looked up at his father and asked, "What's indigestion, Daddy?"

"A bad tummy," Clancy said, "like when you ate too much cheese that time."

Jett's little mouth formed an O. "That was tewwible. I fwowed up weally bad." He smiled again. "Good thing you didn't eat me, Avery. I weally, weally like yowa bwownies."

After that, conversation at the table went on like Clancy and his kids had always been part of the family. When it came time to clear the table, the men took everything to the kitchen, which was as it should be, since the women had prepared the food.

"Want to play a game?" Evie asked the kids.

"Sure," Kenzie said.

Jett was not as convinced. "What game?"

"HiHo Cherry-O."

Jett clapped his hands. "I love HiHo Chewy-O."

"C'mon, then. We have time to play while the guys are cleaning up."

Jett still hesitated. "I don wanna miss dessewt!"

"We won't," Evie assured him, snatching him out of his chair. "They'll call us when all the desserts are on the table."

Jett smiled and patted her cheeks. "I love you almost as much as I love Avery, Evie."

Her sister hugged Jett, then set him on his feet and took his hand and Kenzie's. A moment later, they disappeared into the living room.

Rachel moved over to sit by Avery. "Clancy is a keeper," she whispered.

"I've known him for less than a month, Mom."

"And yet, you invited him and his kids to Thanksgiving dinner."

Avery snuck a look toward the kitchen doorway, then glanced at her mom again. "He asked me to marry him."

"I hope you said yes."

"I didn't. I told him it was too soon."

"What did he say to that?"

"He informed me that his parents only knew each other for two weeks before they got married."

"Dad and I only knew each for six weeks before we tied the knot."

"I know, but I'm not like all of you. I don't jump into things without considering the consequences."

"Have you slept with him yet?"

"Mom!"

"It's an honest question and it deserves an honest answer, honey."

Avery couldn't lie. "All we've done is kiss."

Rachel considered her with an appraising eye. "Are your fingers crossed under the table?"

Avery sighed and held up her hands. "No!"

Her mother smiled. "Well, when you do sleep with him, make sure you use condoms until you're ready to have children."

Avery's face blossomed with color. Did her mother always have to be so straightforward?

Rachel stood. "Better to be practical, Avery." She moved toward the living room. "I'm going to play HiHo Cherry-O. Come join us."

"Give me a minute to digest your advice," Avery said wryly.

Rachel came back and hugged her. "Life is short, honey. When you meet the man of your dreams, you should embrace the moment, grab it, and live out the rest of your life with him." She straightened. "That's all I'm going to say."

As soon as her mother disappeared into the living room, Clancy appeared in the kitchen doorway. "Where are the kids?"

"Playing a game with Mom and Evie."

Clancy nodded, apparently satisfied. She thought he'd go back to the kitchen, but instead, he said, "Since I'm a first-time guest, I'm excused from kitchen clean-up." He rounded the table and held out his hand to her. "Let's take a walk around the block."

Avery didn't argue. While Clancy grabbed their jackets, she stuck her head in the living room. "Clancy and I are going for a walk around the block."

The four people at the coffee table smiled at her.

"Have fun," Evie said. "We'll be fine here without you."

Clancy stood at the front door, waiting for her. He helped her into her jacket, then got into his. He looked around, then kissed her.

Avery almost melted. His kiss offered promises of what lay ahead for them.

Though she could hardly wait, she didn't look forward

to telling him that tonight wasn't going to be the night he thought it was going to be.

CHAPTER 11

THANKSGIVING NIGHT, TIME FOR BED

By the time Clancy pulled into his garage, Jett was sound asleep and Kenzie was doing her best not to nod off. Clancy lowered the garage door and exited the SUV.

"That was the funnest Thanksgiving ever," Kenzie said. "I really like your family, Avery."

Avery smiled and reached over the seat to push several strands of hair off the little girl's face. "I like 'em, too."

"If you married Daddy, we could have more brothers and sisters."

That declaration caught Avery totally off guard. Before she could answer, Clancy opened Jett's door and unbuckled him from his carseat. He gently lifted his son and backed away from the SUV. "I'll be right back to get Kenzie." He winked at Avery, as if sealing some kind of deal.

Kenzie unhooked her seat belt and climbed off her booster seat. "Will you carry me in, Avery? I only weigh a few pounds more than Jett."

"Sure." Avery undid her safety belt and climbed out.

"Are you having a sleepover with Daddy?" Kenzie asked once she was in Avery's arms.

"Uh, no."

"I mean, it's okay if you do. Daddy prob'ly gets lonely sleeping alone." She laid her head on Avery's shoulder and promptly dozed off.

Avery had her doubts about Kenzie's claim that she only weighed a few pounds more than her little brother, but she gave it her all, until she reached the steps leading up to the mudroom. She took the first one and wobbled. While she was trying to get her balance, Clancy appeared in the doorway.

"Didn't you hear me say I'd be back to get Kenzie?"

"She asked me to carry her."

He shook his head at her, amused. "Do you always do what kids ask you to do?"

"I've never been around kids all that much, so I'm not sure what the answer is to that question." She wobbled again and this time lost her balance.

Clancy bolted down the steps, barely stopping her fall.

Kenzie stirred and said, "You should marry Avery, Daddy. Me and Jett want some brothers and sisters."

Again startled and uncomfortable with the child's words, Avery remained silent.

"I swear, I didn't tell her I asked you," Clancy said.

"Did you discuss it with Mo?"

"No."

Stymied, Avery said, "While you were walking around the car to get Jett, she asked me if I was having a sleepover with you. She thinks you get lonely, sleeping alone."

"I haven't been lonely sleeping alone since Mindy left. Now I'm lonely every night, all because I met you. And that's all I'm going to say, in case sleeping children can hear everything, even when they're sleeping." He turned and went into the house.

Avery thought about retrieving her laptop from the back end of his SUV, but decided not to. After that, she debated whether or not to go out the side door and head back to her house, or to go inside and exchange more kisses with Clancy. Before she could decide, there he was, coming down the steps into the garage.

"I know what you're thinking."

"You do?"

"You're considering slinking off in the dark and going back to your place."

She blinked, but didn't say anything.

"That's not going to happen, Avery."

"It's not?"

"No." He walked around to the back end of his SUV to get her laptop.

She couldn't help but notice the bulge behind his zipper. "It's been a long day. Why don't I come back in the morning to work on your IT problem?"

"If that's what you want to do." He slammed the rear lid. "Come inside and help me get the kids in their jammies. We can discuss this further after they're properly tucked in."

It occurred to her that a man saying *jammies* like Clancy did shouldn't be all muscle and steel and sex appeal. "Okay."

He smiled as if he were the cat that had eaten the damned canary and tugged her up the steps.

Inside the mudroom, he said, "I need a kiss to hold me."

Avery melted against him.

A good five minutes later, they walked into the kitchen, where he set her laptop on the counter. Then they moved down the hall, hand-in-hand. Jett was easy to undress and get into his PJs. Kenzie was a little more difficult because she had the pinafore on over her dress, but between the two of them, they managed it.

When they reached the door, Kenzie mumbled, "I hope you have a nice sleepover with Avery, Daddy."

CHAPTER 12

THANKSGIVING NIGHT, ALMOST A SLEEPOVER

Clancy stood frozen in the hallway outside Kenzie's door. "Why does she think we're having a sleepover?"

"Don't ask me."

"You must have some idea."

Avery hazarded a guess. "Walls have ears and kids know everything that's going on?"

He shook his head and looked away. When he looked back, he might as well have had a light bulb shining over his head. "Being her dad, I should've thought of that."

Avery pulled Kenzie's door almost closed.

Clancy stared down at her. "Are you really staying, or are you considering hightailing it home?"

She stared up at him. "I'm going home."

"Damn."

She lifted a shoulder.

He blew out a breath and held out his hand to her.

Avery hesitated and finally took it. She smiled shyly up at him.

"God, you're beautiful."

"I am?"

"Surely you know that."

"I never thought about it, to tell you the truth. I look in the mirror and all I see is plain old me."

They walked down the hall to the bathroom, where he urged her to stand in front of the mirror. "Plain old me needs to take another look at herself and really see what I see every time I look at you."

Avery resisted at first.

"Look, Avery. Really look."

She glanced in the mirror and met his gaze.

"Don't look at me, look at you."

Against her will, she studied her reflection. Was Clancy right? "I'm not beautiful."

He put his hands on her shoulders. "You are, Avery." His hands wandered down to her breasts, fondling them, then moved on to her waist. He grasped the hem of her sweater and tugged it over her head, tossing it on the vanity. "I've never seen breasts as beautiful as yours."

Her gaze sought his again in the mirror. "How can you tell, when I still have my bra on?"

"I just can."

"Seen a lot of breasts, have you?"

"I've seen my fair share, I suppose, but I'm telling you, yours are the most beautiful."

"I want my sweater back on, Clancy."

"No."

She reached for it, anyway, holding it over her breasts.

"Venus de Milo had nothing on you, Avery."

Despite his words, Avery had reservations. She didn't want to ask the question, but it popped out anyway. Damn her insecurities! "Do you only like me because you like my body?"

His expression registered shock. "No!"

"Then why do you like me so much?"

Clancy frowned. "Are you asking me to categorize

*every*thing I like about you?"

That hadn't been the question, but she nodded anyway.

He shook his head. "The list is long, Avery. I like everything about you, including that tiny little mole on your shoulder."

"What's going to happen if we argue?"

"Couples argue. Afterward, they kiss and make up."

That sounded good, except for the arguing part. "I don't like arguments."

"I don't either," he said, then he took the sweater from her hands and tugged it back over her head.

"Will your folks still be at the cabin Sunday night, or are they cutting their trip short this year?"

"They never cut it short." He took his time with her sweater. "I invited them for next week, but Mom said they'll be in the midst of Christmas decorating." His hands moved slowly over her breasts. "She said later in the month would work better."

Avery wondered if they didn't want to meet her.

"I know what you're thinking, and you're way off base. My parents go all out decorating for Christmas. It's a scheduling issue, not an Avery issue."

She took him at his word, hoping he was telling the truth.

It was eight p.m. when Avery woke the first time.

She dozed off again, and went right back into the same dream, featuring Clancy. The next time she awoke, it was almost ten.

The house was quiet, except for Clancy puttering around in the kitchen.

Hellfire and tarnation! How could she have fallen asleep at his house?

Avery tiptoed into the kitchen and quietly slid her laptop off the table. She sighed and took the chicken's way out, sneaking away while he made himself a sandwich with turkey her mom had sent home with him.

She'd snagged her jacket and entered the garage, closing that door quietly behind her before heading to the side door. She opened it, checking to make sure she could get out of his yard through the gate. At her age, fence climbing was a distant memory.

Satisfied, she made sure the door locked behind her and off she went.

Fortunately, she didn't encounter anyone on the way home.

Unfortunately, she remembered her purse was still in Clancy's car.

Fortunately, she had a key to the house hidden in the shed at the back of her property.

Unfortunately, the door to that shed was locked.

Fortunately, her sister Evie had a spare key. Before she called her, all Avery had to do was think up a good reason why she was outside her house, with her laptop, at ten o'clock.

Unfortunately, her phone was in her purse, which was still in Clancy's SUV.

God, she had a lot to learn about sneaking around so she could avoid making love with the man of her dreams.

CHAPTER 13

THE DAY AFTER THANKSGIVING

Clancy had never been quick to wake up, but damn! Avery was in his bed and he needed a lot more love-making with her before he roused his kids.

He reached out, intending to pull her closer to his body and quickly discovered that his need would have to go unfulfilled, because she wasn't in his bed, after all. That's when he realized he'd spent the night *dreaming* about making love with her, not actually *doing* it with her.

Then he remembered that she'd snuck out of his house while he'd made himself a turkey sandwich.

As the song went, Avery was *Gone, Gone, Gone*!

The question was, why had she left? Had he frightened her when he'd pulled off her sweater? In retrospect, that had been a stupid move, but damn! He wanted her. His action had come on the spur of the moment, and without any forethought.

That's what happened when he let his need for her override his common sense!

She must've left because she'd been worried about

Kenzie and Jett, and any questions they'd have at breakfast about her sleeping over with their dad.

On one hand, he couldn't fault Avery for being concerned about that.

On the other hand, he was so hot for her, he almost couldn't see straight. In fact, he needed her so badly, he almost didn't recognize himself. Yeah, he'd been married, but Mindy had never left him in this state. Nor had any of the women he screwed since the divorce, which admittedly, didn't total more than three.

But Avery. My, God! He'd fallen for her the minute she aimed those cornflower-blue eyes of hers at him. Asking her to marry him had come as more of a surprise to him than it had to her, mostly because she hadn't taken him seriously.

He climbed out of bed and moved down the hall, checking Kenzie and Jett. Both slept on soundly.

He headed back to his bedroom and sat on the bed, thinking. Yeah, both the kids would've asked a lot of questions while they ate breakfast, but Avery was quick. She would have made sense of having a sleepover with him somehow.

"You really are a dumb shit," he mumbled into the quiet. There were no explanations to be uttered that would explain why Avery had slept over, except for one, and it wasn't the kind of discussion you had with kids who were five and three.

Daddy wanted to make love to Avery all night long. He could hear their questions now. *What's making love, Daddy? Why do you want to make love to Avery, Daddy? Is that different than kissing, Daddy?*

On that troubling note, Clancy popped up off the bed and headed for the bathroom to take a cold shower.

Too bad it didn't work to tamp down his desire for Avery.

He made a decision, then. Once the kids were up and

dressed, they'd get in the car and go to Avery's. After that, they'd all go to Sugar Plum Cottage for breakfast. If he couldn't have her in his bed, at least he could be *with* her.

Problem solved.

Sort of.

At eight-thirty, both kids were dressed and hungry. Clancy got their jackets on them, then pulled his on and herded them out to the SUV. He got them buckled into their carseats and climbed behind the wheel. The first thing he noticed was Avery's purse on the passenger floorboard.

His thoughts immediately raced to her sitting on her front porch, half-frozen because she didn't have her keys. He reached for the purse and looked inside. Damn! She didn't have her phone, either.

Had she been that anxious to get away from him?

Or, was she running away from her own desire for him?

He preferred to think it was the latter, but he feared it was the former.

If he were being completely honest, if she was running away from herself, that also meant she was running away from him.

"I'll be right back." He climbed out of the SUV and ran back into the house. Her laptop was gone off the table. He mumbled some choice profanities as he went back to the garage. He slammed his hand against the door-opener and climbed back into his SUV.

"Are we going or not, Daddy?" Kenzie asked. "Me and Jett are hungry."

"Yeah, Daddy! I need yams and mawshmallows."

"We're going to breakfast now, and yams and marshmallows is a Thanksgiving thing, Jett."

He backed out of the garage, drove to the corner, turned right, turned right again, and pulled up in Avery's driveway.

"How come Avery didn't have a sleepover with you, Daddy?" Kenzie asked, frowning.

"A sleepova?" Jett asked, surprised. "Why didn't you tell me, Daddy?"

"Grownups don't have to tell kids everything," Kenzie informed him.

"They don't?" her brother asked, looking incredulous. "Is Avery going to bweakfast with us, Daddy?"

"I hope so. You guys wait in the car. I'm taking the key and locking the doors so no one tries to steal you."

They stared at him wide-eyed.

"What should we do if someone tries?" Kenzie asked, her tone worried.

"Honk the horn and keep honking."

She nodded and glanced toward the steering wheel, as if trying to figure out her strategy.

Clancy shut off the engine and climbed out, locking the doors.

"I weally like Avery," Jett said. "I wish she was our mommy."

"I know," Kenzie said with a sigh. "I was hoping a sleepover meant they really liked each other."

"But she didn't sleepova."

"I know, Jett."

"What does it mean if daddy has a fwiend sleepova?"

"They sleep together."

His eyes widened. "They do?" Then he shrugged his small shoulders. "Do they talk, too?"

Kenzie nodded and unhooked her seatbelt. "Probably." She edged over to Jett's side of the car so she could see what was going on at Avery's front door. "They probably kiss a lot, too."

Clancy rang Avery's doorbell, hoping she'd answer. Hell, what if she wasn't even home? Her purse, her keys, and her phone were still his car. Where else could she have gone?

He pressed his ear to the door, then rang the bell again. Were those footsteps?

He straightened and reached for the doorbell one more time. He was about to depress the button when the door opened.

There was Avery, in mulberry-colored sweats, all tousled, looking like she'd just jumped out of his bed after hours of love-making.

"Hi," he said, completely tongue-tied.

"Hi," she said back. "What are you doing here?"

"I came to see if you wanted to join me and the kids for breakfast. We're headed to Sugar Plum Cottage."

"I love Sugar Plum Cottage."

He nodded and his gaze slid over her, lingering on the evidence that she wore no bra beneath the sweatshirt. Apparently, his perusal of her attributes embarrassed her, because she folded her arms over her middle. Did she not know that only seemed to enhance the hardness of her nipples? "Why'd you sneak away?"

"Because."

"That's not an answer."

"I just couldn't stay, okay?"

It wasn't, but what could he say that wouldn't tick her off? He was surprised when she went on.

"I didn't want to face the questions Kenzie and Jett would have at the breakfast table."

"I thought it might be something like that. Your purse is in my car."

"I know. I got a ladder out from behind the shed."

"I suppose you hide a spare key *in* the shed."

"Yes, but no purse, no keys, remember? I drug that stupid ladder over to the house and climbed in a window I'd left unlocked."

"You left a window unlocked?"

"I know, my bad. I won't make that mistake again." She sucked in a breath. "I'm sorry I snuck away." Her long eyelashes swept down, touching her cheeks, then she looked up.

"If you'd marry me, you wouldn't have to do any more sneaking."

She sighed.

"I take it, you're still not convinced."

"I'm considering your proposal, Clancy."

"Can you consider harder…and faster?"

"No."

"Did you hurt yourself climbing through the window?"

"A little, but I'll live."

"Do you need doctoring? I'm pretty good at it."

"I'm sure you are."

She licked her lips, reminding him that he really wanted to kiss her again. "I've been thinking about our relationship, Avery."

"Oh? What did you come up with?"

"I've never felt like this before. That's why I know I love you."

She dropped her arms and clasped her hands behind her. "Are sweats okay for Sugar Plum Cottage?"

"If you put on a bra under your sweatshirt." He knew he shouldn't have, but he ogled her again. "I don't want other guys daydreaming about you because they can see your nipples."

"I am wearing a bra," she informed him, crossing her arms over her chest this time."They must be responding to the cold air."

He nodded like an idiot.

"Aren't your kids waiting in the car?"

He started, as if he'd forgotten he even had kids. "Yeah, they are."

"I'll get my jacket." She turned away and limped toward the mudroom..

"You *did* hurt yourself."

"Just a little. I have a cut on my knee and a scratch on my palm."

He reached out and grasped her arm gently, forcing her to face him. "Let me see."

She turned and held up her hand. An inch-long scratch ran beneath her two middle fingers.

"What about your knee?"

"It'll be fine. I cleaned both wounds with hydrogen peroxide after I took a shower."

Clancy didn't quite believe her knee was fine, considering she was limping. "I want to see your knee."

She tilted her head at him. "Since when did you become a doctor?"

"Since I was a medic in the Marines."

Her eyes widened. "You were?"

"One thing you should know about me, Avery. I don't lie. Ever."

"Good to know." She turned and limped the rest of the way to mudroom, where she sat on the bench and pulled up her sweatpants so he could have a look at her knee.

"It looks like you might need a couple of stitches."

"I'm not going to get stitches."

"Then put a butterfly bandage on it."

"I don't have any."

He frowned. "I'll go buy some. Okay to leave the kids here while I go to the drugstore?"

"Why can't we hit the drugstore on the way to Sugar Plum Cottage?"

"We could." He smirked. "Do you have an alternative

solution for everything?"

"Yes, it makes life easier." She lowered the leg of her sweatpants and stood. She pulled her jacket off the hook and said, "I'm ready."

"Uh, do you need to comb your hair or brush your teeth?"

She shook her head in disgust and limped down to the bathroom. When she returned minutes later, she looked all put together, but he really missed her tousled look.

"Can I give you a good morning kiss?"

She hesitated, then said, "If you want to."

"I do." And then he laid a whopper on her. When he finished, he almost uttered the I-love-you words again, but decided, in this case, silence would be his key to success.

CHAPTER 14

BREAKFAST AT SUGAR PLUM COTTAGE

At the Sugar Plum Cottage, Jett told his father exactly what he wanted. "Fwench toast, little sausages, OJ, and stwabewwies, please."

Avery thought the three-year-old was adorable as he pointed to the picture on the menu, and he was so polite about it, too.

Kenzie, on the other hand, couldn't make up her mind if she wanted a breakfast sandwich, blueberry pancakes, or French toast, like her brother had ordered. Finally, she decided to duplicate his order, but added, "I'd also like milk, please."

"Me, too!" Jett cried.

"Two milks, coming up," the server said with a smile. "How about you, ma'am?"

"What the kids are having sounds good, but I'll have coffee, instead of milk."

"You want that in the kid's size, or the grownup size?"

"How many pieces of French toast in the grownup size?"

"Four."

Avery didn't hesitate. "Grownup, please."

The server nodded. "How 'bout you, Clancy?"

Avery did a double-take. How often did Clancy bring his kids and/or significant others to the Sugar Plum Cottage, that the server knew him by his first name?

Clancy smiled at the server and ordered the Alpha-Man Breakfast.

Avery wasn't surprised. Clancy struck her as a man who had big appetites for everything.

After they ate, he took the route home that followed Sugar Plum Creek.

"Can we go fishing, Daddy?" Jett asked.

"It's not fishing season," Clancy told him.

The boy's lower lip quivered. "How come?"

"It's too cold," Kenzie said.

Jett glanced out the side window. "Is it gonna snow?"

"It might," Kenzie replied. "We can make a snowman, if it does."

Jett clapped his hands and yelled, "Yaaaaay!"

"What's on your agenda for the rest of the day?" Clancy asked Avery.

"I need to finish up the job I started on Wednesday, but other than that, not much." She slid a side glance at him. "Don't you have a conference call at eleven?"

He nodded, then turned a heated glance on her.

Avery squirmed in her seat and bit her bottom lip.

"Don't make promises you can't keep," Clancy said.

Her eyes widened and her face got extremely warm, which made him grin.

"Mo's taking the kids to see a Disney flick this afternoon."

"She is?" Kenzie asked from the rear seat. "Which one?"

"*The Little Mermaid*," Clancy said. "That's your favorite, isn't it?"

Kenzie nodded enthusiastically.

"I like the movie 'bout caws better," Jett said.

"If you're really good, she might take you to see that on Sunday," Clancy said, looking all innocent.

"Why?" Kenzie asked. "We've got *Cars* on DVD."

Avery smirked. "So much for planning ahead."

"I am slightly deficient in that area," Clancy admitted.

"Who wants caramel corn?" Avery asked, changing the subject.

"Me! Me!" came cries from the back seat.

She glanced at Clancy. "There's a little shop up ahead on the left that has the best caramel corn ever. Can we stop?"

"We just had breakfast," he protested.

"Daddy!" two kids wailed from the back seat.

Kenzie added, "Me and Jett love caramel corn."

"Okay, already." He signaled to make a left turn, then parked in front of Sugar Plum Goodies. Before he knew it, both kids and Avery had their seatbelts undone.

"Can we buy some candy to take to *The Little Mewmaid*?"

Clancy shook his head. "See what you've done?" he asked Avery.

"What? Everyone loves candy and caramel corn."

His eyes lowered to study her mouth, then he lifted his gaze again, and finally, he glanced at the back seat. "Remember your manners when we go into the candy shop, okay?"

The little ones nodded solemnly.

"My treat," Avery said.

"What time is Auntie Mo coming?" Kenzie asked.

"Eleven," Clancy said, and glanced at his watch. He had the conference call from eleven to one, then he'd have Avery all to himself. "She's taking you for hot dogs after the movie, then to the fun center."

"Yaaaaay!" Jett said, clapping again. "I love hot dogs! And the fun centa!"

Deficient at planning ahead, my ass, Avery thought. Clancy would probably get an A+ if such a class was ever offered.

Mo arrived at Clancy's house at eleven straight up. The movie started at 11:20 and would run an hour and twenty-three minutes. Afterward, they'd go to Hot Dog Heaven, and after they ate, they'd hit Chuckles Fun Center. "Don't count on seeing us again until five o'clock."

Clancy put the phone on MUTE and nodded. "If Jett gets tired, he may fall asleep during the movie."

"No, I won't!" his son protested. "We gots some candy at Sugaw Plum Goodies, Auntie Mo."

"Did you get some for me, too?" Mo asked, squatting down to put Jett's jacket on him. "I love Milk Duds."

Jett nodded with enthusiasm. "That's what we gotted you." He slapped his hands against his aunt's cheeks. "Let's go!"

Mo straightened and took Jett's hand. "You two have fun while we're gone."

By the twinkle in Mo's eye, Avery figured Mo thought she knew exactly what they were going to have fun doing after his conference call. She hated to burst Mo's bubble, but she had to say it. "I'm going to be working on a technical issue Clancy's IT department is having."

Right on cue, Mo looked surprised. "You are?"

Avery nodded. "Louise is taking care of her husband and she can't deal with the problem herself, so I volunteered to help."

Mo glanced at her brother, who had half an ear to his conference call and half an ear to the conversation between her and Avery. "I see."

Clancy muted the phone again. "Be good, both of you."

"We're always good, Daddy," Kenzie said, which made Jett giggle.

Clancy waved them off, then Avery passed him, following them. He muted the phone one more time. "Where are you going?"

"Home to finish my project. Call when your conference call is done. I'll come back and work on your IT problem."

Clancy would've rather had her stay right where she was, but for now, she was running away again and he had to live with it. "Okay."

Mo turned and winked at her brother, then said to Avery, "I like you, Avery. You're a take-charge kind of woman."

Avery wasn't so sure about that, but she was definitely a woman who couldn't sit around doing nothing…and thinking about what Clancy had in mind, once he hung up the phone.

Clancy frowned. He was having a hard time focusing on his conference call, when all he could think about was Avery. He wondered why she couldn't complete her work at his house, then he remembered she hadn't brought her laptop along.

He closed and locked the door and unmuted his phone. "Sorry," he said. "My kids were just leaving and I missed the last thirty seconds. Would you mind repeating what you just said?"

No one grumbled about his request, probably because they all had kids, too.

Wishing he were in bed with Avery instead of on a damned conference call, he made his way back to his home office.

The next two hours seemed like an eternity, but at

1:15, he signed off and called Avery. "I'm done."

"I'll come back over around two. I'm almost finished with my project."

"I'll be waiting."

His long legs carried him down the hall to his bedroom wishing there was a naked Avery waiting for him on the bed. He sighed. She'd be ringing the doorbell soon. Would she be more eager to get naked with him this time?

Hopeful, he checked to make sure the bedroom was as neat as he could get it, then he went back to the living room, staring out the window.

At two o'clock straight up, the doorbell chimed.

He flung the door open, expecting Avery, but it was the paperboy, coming to collect for the month.

Avery walked up the sidewalk behind him. "Hi."

She looked so beautiful, Clancy found himself tongue-tied again. "Hi."

"Hi, Bobby."

"Hi, Avery. You sure you don't want to subscribe to *Creekside News*?"

She smiled at the boy. "Positive, but thanks for asking." She aimed her smile at Clancy and entered the house.

"I'll grab my checkbook," Clancy said, heading back to his home office. Less than five minutes later, he traipsed back down the hall.

He glanced around the room and there Avery was, standing at the window, watching the snow fall.

"You changed your clothes."

"I did."

"Why?"

"Sweats are unprofessional, and I'm here to work."

"Hunh. I forgot there was a reason why you brought your laptop with you."

She raised an eyebrow at him.

"I can't stop thinking about you, Avery."

She got a funny look on her face, then as suddenly as it was there, it was gone. "I can't stop thinking about you, either."

"I love you."

Avery might have said the same thing back to him, but Clancy's intense expression drove all thought from her mind. Still, she managed to ask, "Can I have one kiss before we start?"

"You can have as many kisses as you want."

"One will do me for now. We have work to do, remember?"

From the look on his face, that reminder might have been the equivalent to a bucket of cold water over his head.

CHAPTER 15

SUNDAY AFTER THANKSGIVING

Clancy knocked on Avery's front door, his anticipation so palpable, he was afraid he might come in his boxers.

When she didn't answer right away, he knocked again. Finally, he realized she might not be able to hear him unless he rang the doorbell. Before he could press it, the door opened.

There stood Avery, looking for all the world like a woman ready to be loved, except that she had a dab of brownie batter on her nose and a wooden spoon in her hand. She smiled at him. "Hi."

"Hi." He stepped into the house, kicked the door closed with his foot, and gathered her in his arms so he could kiss her.

The days since Friday had seemed like months to him. "I missed you."

"I missed you, too. I'm baking brownies."

He nodded and kissed her again, and again. And again. The oven beeped.

"The oven's ready. The brownies are ready to go in."

"When are you going to marry me?"

"I'm still considering your proposal.'

He wiped the batter off the tip of her nose and licked his finger.

She waved her wooden spoon as if it were actually a magic wand and smiled at him again.

Before he knew it, she was out of his arms and walking back toward the kitchen. He hurried after her, enjoying the sway of her hips in denim jeans.

She set the spoon in the mixing bowl and slid the pan of brownies into the oven. After that, she set the timer. "Want to help me clean up?"

"I'd rather take you to bed."

That's what Avery wanted, too, but she hadn't convinced herself it was the right thing to do. Instead, she gathered the dirty dishes, setting them in the sink. "Notice anything different today?"

Clancy gave the kitchen a cursory glance. "No."

She *tsk-tsked* and turned on the water to run it into the mixing bowl.

She was so mesmerizing, he couldn't pull his gaze away from her.

"Are you sure?"

He glanced around again. Then he got it. Twinkle was missing. "Where's your dog?"

Avery shook her head and turned back to scrubbing the brownie-mixing dishes before she loaded them into the dishwasher.

He looked around again. "I give up. What's different?"

"I put up my Christmas wreath."

He glanced around and spied the wreath on what had been a bare wall between the kitchen and the living room. "It looks nice there."

"Thank you. I made that wreath myself."

He gave it a second look. "Nice." Clancy decided to take a chance. He approached her backside and slid his arms around her.

She looked over her shoulder at him and smiled yet again. "I can't wipe down the counter with your arms around me."

"You can't?" For some reason known only to space aliens, he took that as approval to move his hands up over her breasts.

"Clancy, don't."

"Why? Don't you like what I'm doing?"

She glanced at the timer. "It's not that I don't like it," she said, her breaths coming a little faster, "but I'm baking."

"You strike me as being a multi-tasker."

She nodded and leaned back against him. "I'm a great multi-tasker, but I can't think when you're doing what you're doing."

"I want to do a lot more than this."

"I know, but that's not going to happen."

"You're torturing me, Avery."

"You're torturing both of us, Clancy."

He squeezed her nipples once, then dropped his hands and backed away.

"We'll have time for more kissing after I finish cleaning up…and before the timer buzzes."

"Kissing is good," he admitted, "but I want all of you, Avery, not just your mouth."

Avery wet the dish cloth and proceeded to wipe down the countertop.

"Aren't you going to say anything?"

She finished what she was doing, then rinsed out the cloth and folded it over the sink divider. "What do you want me to say?"

Clancy knew he had to choose the right words, but for

some reason, nothing came to him, or at least, not the words he wanted to utter. All he could think of in the moment was, "Do you always have to answer a question with another question?"

Avery checked the three vanilla-scented candles burning in the kitchen. As ploys went, it was transparent as hell. "I never really thought about it, but now that I *do* think about it, the answer is yes."

Clancy stared down at her. "Want to play the question game?"

She made a face. "That doesn't sound like much fun."

"It can be."

"Who asks the first question?"

"You."

"Okay." She appeared to think for a moment, then she said, "I've read that men and women don't reach orgasm at the same time. Is that true?"

Clancy's jaw literally dropped. "Why didn't I know you were thinking about sex?"

"I have no idea, but aren't you supposed to answer my question, not ask one of your own?"

He shrugged his wide shoulders.

"You started the game," she reminded him. "And I don't have to be thinking about sex to ask a question about sex, do I?"

"You're answering a question with a question again."

She laughed softly. "I can't help myself."

"In answer to your question, I have no idea. I think if a man and a woman are in sync, if they're completely compatible, they can have an orgasm at the same time."

"Hmm."

"Does that *hmm* mean you'll marry me?"

"I'm not one to rush when it comes to making decisions, Clancy."

"So I noticed," he responded, his tone both wry and disappointed.

"Tell me about your wife."

"Why? She's not part of my life anymore."

"I want to know everything about you, and that includes your ex-wife."

"Tell me about your old boyfriends first, then I'll tell you about Mindy."

"I don't really have any old boyfriends."

"Liar," he accused in a gentle tone.

"No, really. I had a few dates in high school, and one guy gave me my first kiss when I was a senior, but other than that, I didn't really."

"C'mon, Avery, you're beautiful. Who wouldn't want to date you?"

"I didn't say guys didn't want to date me," she said.

"So, what? You chose not to date?"

"I didn't say that, either."

"Then what are you saying?"

"Maybe I've been waiting for the right man to come along." She sucked in her cheeks. "Also, my two brothers might have deterred guys from asking me out."

He couldn't seem to let the first part of her statement go. "Am I the right man, Avery?"

"Do you think I'd let you kiss me and fondle my boobs if you weren't?"

That cinched it for Clancy. "All you need to know about Mindy is that she didn't love me or the kids and she took off. End of story."

CHAPTER 16

DECEMBER 1, CHRISTMAS DECORATING

Avery lugged in bags and boxes from her SUV. After saving all year to decorate her new home for Christmas, she was excited to get started.

Santa would be flying in twenty-four days from today and she wanted everything to look as Christmasy as possible for him and the reindeer, not to mention Kenzie, Jett, and Clancy.

Everything she'd purchased was laid out on the living room floor, but that was okay. This was her first Christmas in her new home. It had gone from being slightly shoddy six months ago, to a real gem now. She had a right to splurge, if she wanted to. She'd worked hard to earn her money, after all.

Her doorbell sounded just as she opened the last package. She smiled. Clancy and his kids were picking her up so they could go shopping for a Christmas tree.

She flung open the door, expecting to see their happy faces. Instead, she found a box on her porch, addressed to her, but with no return address. That meant it hadn't been delivered via the USPS, or FedEx, or even UPS.

In today's world, no one in their right mind opened a package with no return address on it. What if there was a bomb inside? Or a poisonous snake? Or a herd of rabid bats?

Now that she didn't have that figured out, she tried to decide what to do with the box. After five minutes of staring at it, and letting all the warm air inside the house, outside the house, she sighed and picked up the box off the front porch and carried it to the garage.

Maybe Clancy could tell her what to do with it.

She went back to sorting Christmas decorating goodies. Ornaments with ornaments. Tabletop décor with tabletop décor. Wall stuff with wall stuff. Thirty minutes later, the doorbell rang again.

This time, Avery peeked out the front window.

Clancy and his kids stood on the porch, waiting with obvious impatience for her to open the door.

Excited, because she'd never shopped for a Christmas tree before, she was even more excited that she'd be shopping for one with Clancy, Jett, and Kenzie.

She hurried to the door and opened it. "Hi."

"Get yowa coat on, Avery," Jett screamed. "We gots to get a good twee!"

Avery grinned at him. "I don't think we'll miss out, sweetie."

"Daddy says we might," Jett responded with a frown.

Avery leveled her gaze on Clancy. "Really?"

"Really. Get your coat. We don't want to be late." His eyes twinkled, which let her know he was putting on a show for his three-year-old.

"I should comb my hair, and use the bathroom…."

"Hurry," Kenzie urged. "Last year we were late and all the good trees were almost gone."

"You lost a tooth!" Avery said, staring at Kenzie's smile.

"I was brushing my teeth this morning and it just fell

out," Kenzie said with a grin. "Daddy says the Tooth Fairy will take my tooth and leave some money under my pillow tonight."

"Lucky you! Do you have a Tooth Fairy pillow?"

Kenzie nodded. "I put the tooth in the pocket and stuck it under my pillow."

"The Tooth Faiwy needs to visit me," Jett said. "I like money."

Clancy laughed.

Avery would've explained her messy house, but it was apparent they weren't interested. Getting to the tree lot took top priority, along with losing baby teeth, and having the Tooth Fairy visit. "I'll be out lickety-split."

The two little ones frowned up at her.

Clancy, on the other hand, perused her body from head-to-toe, lingering a little longer on her breasts. When he looked up to meet her gaze, he said, "Baby, it's cold outside."

She knew darned good and well her nipples had hardened because of the cold air. She stepped back and closed the door on the three of them, then went to grab her coat and purse.

Minutes later, she left the house, locking the door behind her, and made her way to the driveway. She came to an abrupt halt when she encountered the dual-cab truck, cherry red in color, parked in her driveway.

Clancy stood at the passenger door, waiting to help her up into the cab. "You look hot," he whispered in her ear.

She had on a teal-colored sweater and blue jeans. How hot could that be? Did it even matter, if Clancy liked what he saw? "Thank you." Belatedly, she realized he might have been talking about her internal temperature, not the clothes she wore. "When did you have time to buy a truck?"

"Last night. Do you like it?"

"It's big. And red."

He laughed. "I take it that's a yes."

Avery glanced up, nodding.

"We're picking up a pizza after we get the trees," Clancy said.

"Sounds yummy."

"Can you come for dinner tomorrow tonight?"

She smiled, wondering if his question masked a double entendre. "I wouldn't miss your 'sketti and meatballs."

He blew out a sigh of relief.

Avery changed the subject with a question of her own. "Did I mention that I've never shopped for a Christmas tree before?"

He stared at her in disbelief. "That can't be right."

She raised her right hand. "I swear. Mom never took us kids because she said she couldn't concentrate with four hellions scrambling around, knocking over trees. She waited until we'd gone off to school, then she hit the tree lot. By the time we got home, it would be mostly decorated."

"That's harsh."

Avery shrugged. "I never did much for Christmas when I lived in an apartment, especially because we always had a big blowout at the folks' house. Now that I have my own place, I went out and bought decorations."

"You're putting me on, right?"

"Why would I do that?"

His expression grew somber. "You're serious?"

"As serious as Rudy's red nose."

"Maybe we should help you decorate your tree first."

"As I started to say earlier, I have decorations all over the house. I don't even know what I'm doing, so I'm not sure having you and the kids help me decorate my tree is a good idea the first time out."

"We could sit on the sofa and supervise you," he said, trying not to smile.

"I'm sure."

Kenzie rolled down her window. "Daddy, we're gonna be late!"

"Okay, honey." He looked back at Avery. "You can sit on our couch and watch us. We'll show you how it's done, and after the kids go to bed—"

"Don't say it!" Even though she'd stopped him from saying what he wanted to say, Avery got all hot and bothered thinking about what could've come after decorating the tree, if not for her inner reluctance to commit.

"Your face matches my truck," Clancy noted. "Is that because you're thinking about what you wouldn't let me say...or something else?"

"That's for me to know and you never to find out."

A big grin split his face. "So, we *are* on the same wavelength."

Avery blinked at him, desperate to change the subject, but she couldn't come up with another topic to discuss that didn't involve what he was obviously thinking about.

The four of them decided to eat the pizza at Pizza King. It was just after noon and no one else was in the restaurant, if you didn't count the boisterous gathering in the party room.

On the drive to Clancy's place afterward, Kenzie and Jett chattered nonstop about the ornaments that went on the tree. Avery was a little envious that she didn't have any ornaments from her childhood to hang on her tree.

"Listen up," Clancy said. "Here's how this is going to go. I'll get the tree out of the bed of the truck and take it into the garage, where I'll put it in the tree stand. While I'm doing that, Kenzie can show Avery our ornaments. She and Jett can only reach halfway up the tree, so when I bring it in, they'll tell us where they want them placed on the higher branches."

Avery listened and nodded. Not only had she never been Christmas tree shopping before, but she'd also never decorated a tree before. Did she dare admit that?

"Avery?"

"What?"

"Are you paying attention?"

"Absolutely." She smiled at Clancy, hoping he wouldn't know she was lying.

"Then why are you frowning?"

Caught, darn it!

"Uh...did I remember to tell you that I've never decorated a tree, either?"

"What?" came the appalled young voices from the back seat.

Clancy gave her a second look. "Not ever?"

She shook her head.

"Do you even celebrate Christmas?"

"Sure, but since Mom and Dad always make a big deal of it, I never did more than put a wreath up on the wall." She added, "The one I showed you?"

Clancy shook his head. "You have a lot to learn, Avery."

"I'm a quick study," she informed him, and immediately wanted to recall her words.

He shot her a sexy smile. "I'm sure you are."

"Do I have to do anything special before I can decorate my tree?"

"Just follow my lead," Clancy said. "There are so many things I can teach you."

Curious, because she knew he wasn't talking about Christmas trees, she asked, "Like what?"

He gave her a sizzling glance. "For that, my love, you will have to wait and see."

CHAPTER 17

AFTER THE KIDS ARE ASLEEP

Clancy kissed Avery all the way down the hall. It took him five minutes to reach the doorway of his bedroom. He kicked the door shut and locked it, then kissed her all the way to the bed.

A moment later, she looked around. "How'd we get to your bedroom?"

"The usual way."

"You know I'm not ready, Clancy."

"When will you be ready?"

"I'm not sure."

"I can help you figure it out."

She was pretty sure she knew how that would go. "I have to figure it out on my own."

"Let me know if you want my help."

She stared up at him. "What kind of help could you give me?"

His gaze roamed over her body, then back up again. "I'm pretty good at getting clothes off."

"My clothes are just fine where they are."

"I'm also good at...." He trailed off and cocked his

head. "One of the kids is up." He straightened and moved toward the door, which he opened. Kenzie and Jett both stood in the hall. "What's wrong?" he asked them.

"Jett has a tummy ache."

"Too much candy," Clancy muttered.

"Is Avery still hewa?" Jett asked.

Clancy looked over his shoulder, then stepped aside so Jett could see her.

"Will you wock me, Avery? That always makes my tummy feel betta."

"Sure," Avery said. She popped up off of Clancy's bed and beelined for his son. She picked him up and carried him to the living room, where the rocker was.

"Where are you going?" Clancy asked Kenzie.

"Jett always likes me nearby when he's got a tummy ache."

Clancy knew that to be true.

Resigned to rescheduling his plans to seduce Avery, he followed the three of them down the hall to the living room.

Two hours later, Jett's tummy ache was gone and he was ready to head back to his bed.

Clancy scooped him out of Avery's arms and carried him to his bedroom. Several minutes later, he did the same with Kenzie, who'd fallen asleep on the floor.

When he came back to the living room, Avery was putting on her coat. "Where are you going?"

"Home."

"It's two a.m., Avery. I don't want you out walking at this time of the night."

"It's not that far."

He shook his head.

She could tell by his demeanor, he was dead serious.

"I'm not sleeping in your bed, Clancy."

"You don't have to. We have a spare bedroom. You can sleep there."

She'd forgotten it was a four-bedroom house.

"Well?"

"I'm thinking."

"About what?"

"Will you promise to stay in your bedroom?"

He raised his hand. "Scout's honor."

"Were you ever a Boy Scout?"

"For a brief period of time."

She thought some more and finally made up her mind. "Okay."

"Good."

He hustled over to her. "How about a good night kiss?"

"I suppose that would be all right."

"Thank God."

Five minutes later, Avery headed for the guest bedroom. She closed the door and laid on the bed for a long time, thinking about Clancy, wondering what it would be like to make love with him.

What if she got pregnant? What then?

Would he want her to get an abortion? Would he tell her to walk away and never look back? Or, would he welcome another child and love it like he loved Jett and Kenzie?

That brought to mind his marriage proposal and his declaration of love. Had he been serious about both?

She sighed and turned to look at the clock on the bedside table. Four a.m.

In some ways, she felt like a straggler, left behind by all her friends, who'd experienced sex at a much earlier age.

She had so much catching up to do!

And then she remembered Twinkle. Poor dog was

probably suffering from not being let outside to do his business.

She crept out of the spare bedroom and went to the bathroom down the hall. A few minutes later, she opened the door and found Jett and Kenzie sitting in the hallway, staring up at her.

"Aren't you having a sleepover with Daddy?" Kenzie asked.

Avery was eternally grateful that she had all her clothes on and had brushed her hair into some semblance of looking normal. "No," she said. "I need to get home and take care of Twinkle."

"Can we come with you?" Jett asked, rubbing his eyes.

"Not this time." She held out her hands to Clancy's two beautiful children. "I'll tuck you both back in, then I need to go."

"Will you come fowa 'sketti dinnew tonight?"

"If your dad still wants me here, I'll be here."

"He will," Kenzie assured her. "When you marry him, can we call you Mommy?"

Caught off guard by the question, Avery said, "You're getting ahead of yourself."

Kenzie shook her head and her lower lip jutted out. "I heard Daddy ask you to marry him."

"You did? When?"

"The first time you came to 'sketti dinner."

God, walls *did* have ears! "He was kidding."

"Daddy doesn't kid about stuff like that," Jett said, sounding about ten years older than he was.

"He doesn't?"

They both shook their heads emphatically.

"Daddy always says, the next time he gets the love bug, it will be forever," Kenzie said. "If he asked you, he meant it, and he wasn't kidding."

Avery changed the subject. "Did the Tooth Fairy visit you last night, Kenzie?"

Kenzie smiled up at her. "She sure did, and she left me a five dollar bill."

"Wow." The value of baby teeth had gone up since Avery had lost hers.

On that note, the bedroom door at the end of the hall opened and there stood Clancy, in his boxer shorts, looking for all hell like a Greek god.

Avery forgot all about the Tooth Fairy and baby teeth.

"Leaving so soon?" he asked in that sexy voice of his.

"She has to go home and take care of Twink," Kenzie said.

"Don't you want Avery to have a sleepova with you, Daddy?" Jett asked.

Clancy's long strides carried him down the hall, where he knelt down and said to his kids. "I want what Avery wants, and if she has to go home to take care of Twinkle, then she has to go home and take care of Twinkle." He looked up at her. "You'll be back for 'sketti, won't you?"

Avery nodded, trying hard to meet his gaze. Damn! Why'd he have to come out of his bedroom in nothing but boxer shorts?

"Yaaaaay!" Jett screamed, clapping his little hands.

"Are you scared to walk home by yourself?" Kenzie asked.

Avery looked down at her. "No." She glanced at Clancy, who stared at her with such hunger, she knew she'd probably regret walking out his front door.

Still, a girl did what a girl had to do.

CHAPTER 18

SUNDAY, JUST BEFORE 'SKETTI NIGHT

The first thing Avery did when she got home was tell Twinkle about her evening at the O'Rourkes. After she let her dog outside, she headed to her bedroom to undress, then she stepped into the bathroom, intent on taking a shower.

She turned sideways in front of the mirror and imagined herself pregnant with Clancy's child. She laid her hand against her abdomen. How big would she get? Would it be a boy or a girl, or maybe even twins? A couple of sighs later, she stepped under the shower head and washed her hair and her body. After she wiped down the glass, she wrapped a towel around her head and used another one to dry.

A chill wracked her body and she realized it wasn't quite five a.m. It was snowing outside on this cold December morning and her heat hadn't kicked on yet.

As she climbed into her polar bear PJs, she wondered if Clancy would invite her to his bedroom again after 'sketti dinner. Surely, they could lie on his bed and do nothing but kiss, right?

She made a sound of disbelief, knowing that if they laid on his bed, it would be for far more than kissing.

She'd better make up her mind pretty darned quick.

The thought of facing the rest of her life without Clancy in it was so dismal, so disturbing, she could've cried.

When the doorbell rang a few hours later, Avery knew it must be Clancy and the kids, delivering her Christmas tree. She climbed out of bed, but didn't bother to pull on a robe as she hurried to the front door.

She flung it open, excited about the prospect of seeing the man she hadn't even known existed before Halloween. The man she loved beyond a shadow of a doubt. The man who had two beautiful kids. The man who would help make siblings for Jett and Kenzie.

"Hi," she said, feeling a little shy for some reason.

"Hi," he said back. His gaze ran a lazy path down her body, then back up again. "I have your tree. I thought you might need it to decorate."

All of a sudden, she wanted to drag him down the hall to her bedroom.

Now, where had *that* come from?

Then she realized he didn't have Jett and Kenzie with him. "Where are the kids?"

"At home, with Mo. They're making cookies."

"Cookies."

He nodded. "Christmas cookies. 'Tis the season, you know."

"I might have heard that somewhere…."

"I know I've said this before, but I can't stop thinking about you, Avery."

"I can't stop thinking about you, either."

"That's good. I want you to think about me all the time."

She quirked her lips. "Believe me, I do."

"I'll bring your tree in, so it can warm up."

"Why does it need to warm up?"

"Because, it does." His gaze raked her body again. "Maybe we can talk while it's warming up."

Speechless, she nodded.

He gave her a sexy smile. "So, we're in agreement?"

She nodded again and reached for the top button of her pajama top. When she realized she'd been thinking of unbuttoning *all* the buttons, she dropped her hand. "The stand is in the living room."

He grabbed the tree from its leaning position against the house, then stepped up into the foyer and headed for the living room.

Avery shut and locked the door and headed down the hall to her bedroom, intent on getting dressed.

Moments later, Clancy stood in her bedroom doorway, staring at her. "You have a beautiful body."

Avery hadn't even realized she'd left her door open, and she also didn't know what to say in response to Clancy's compliment except, "Thank you," and even that came out sounding strangled.

He stepped into her bedroom and advanced on her. "I want to touch you, Avery."

Did she let him, or not? Uncertain, she gave him a slight nod, thankful she'd already put on her bra and briefs..

He ran his hand over breasts, teasing her nipples as he stroked her.

She savored his touch.

Then his other hand cupped her bottom, beneath her briefs.

"What are you doing, Clancy?"

"Touching you," he whispered against her lips, and then he kissed her.

Avery clutched his sweatshirt, both because she didn't

want to fall, and she didn't know what else to do with her hands.

So many sensations washed through her, but she couldn't focus on a single one of them. All she knew for certain was that she liked what he was doing to her breasts and she liked the way he kneaded her buttocks.

When his mouth left hers, it traveled a path down her neck to her breasts. He kissed his way across the skin exposed by the bra, and then the cups sprang apart and his mouth was on her nipples, sucking, nipping, kissing.

She wanted to tell him to stop, but it all felt so good, she couldn't find the words.

Somehow, her bra ended up on the floor and she and Clancy ended up on her bed. She let him continue adoring her breasts, and then his mouth travelled across her belly. Suddenly, her briefs were being lowered.

All Avery knew for sure was that his ultimate goal was the womanly part of her at the juncture of her thighs. It took her a moment, but she finally grasped his head and forced him to look at her. "Don't, Clancy."

"Why? This is what we're made for."

She had no doubt of that, but.... God, why couldn't she think?

Suddenly, her briefs were sliding down her legs and Clancy was kissing her belly again. "Don't stop me, Avery. This is for both of us."

Her breath came so furiously, she couldn't speak.

"What are you....?"

And then his mouth landed between her legs and Avery was lost.

An hour later, they wandered into the living room to straighten the tree. Avery was naked as the day she was born and Clancy had discarded his sweatshirt, jeans, and boots. She thought he looked manly in his tee shirt and boxers. And socks.

"It's not quite ready," he said.

"It looks ready to me."

"But you're not the expert. Wanna go back to your bedroom for a while?"

She stared up at him, wondering exactly what he had in mind. "Okay."

"I never knew sex could be this good," Clancy said, nibbling on her breast once they were back in her bed.

"I didn't either," Avery admitted, enjoying having his mouth right where it was. "Is it because we love each other?"

"It's love, and we're sexually compatible, which is why I want you to marry me."

"We don't really know each other," she said, "and how do you know we're sexually compatible?"

"I just do, okay? I love you, you love me. We'll have more kids and live happily ever after."

"Is that the way you felt about Mindy when you first got married?" Avery asked, not realizing her question would be a deal breaker.

"I never felt like this with or about Mindy, Avery." He pushed away from her and out of the bed. Before she knew what was happening, he was halfway dressed again.

She raised up on her elbows. "What did I say to make you angry?"

He stopped buttoning his shirt and looked at her with a fierce expression. "I don't like having an inquisition aimed at me about Mindy."

"It wasn't an inquisition. I merely asked a question."

He looked away then finished buttoning his shirt. "I need to get home. The cookies are probably done by now and my kitchen's probably a mess."

"Clancy?"

He stuck his feet into his boots and grabbed his jacket.

Without another word, he went down the hall and left through the front door, slamming it behind him.

Stunned without understanding exactly why her question had pissed off the man she loved, Avery curled up in a ball on the bed.

She obviously had a lot to learn about relationships, but weren't you supposed to be able to talk over any subject with the man you were in love with, even if it concerned his ex-wife?

Her parents had always told her when you found the man you wanted to spend the rest of your life with, make sure you could discuss anything with him, from the price of wheat in Russia, to the man in the moon, to exactly how you liked your lovemaking.

Well, they hadn't used those words exactly, but it was something similar, and Avery knew what they'd meant.

She'd really gone and gotten herself into a fine pickle! This was exactly what stupid insecurities did to you. They left you feeling sorry for yourself!

Should she lay in bed and cry all day, trying to figure things out?

Or should she get dressed and decorate the tree, trying to figure things out?

And if she *did* happen to figure out things (or even if she didn't), was she still invited to 'sketti night?

CHAPTER 19

'SKETTI DINNER. . .OR SKIP DINNER?

Avery left her house at 4:45 p.m. It wouldn't take long to reach Clancy's house, since it was just around the corner, but as slow as she was moving, she might not knock on his door until 5:15, or even 5:30.

Either way, she'd be late for 'sketti and meatballs, which would probably piss Clancy off even more than he was already pissed at her.

At the corner, Avery let out a long sigh. She turned left and took another step.

Half-way down to the middle of the block where Clancy's house was located, with her doubts knocking her brain and her heart around like crazy, she seriously considering heading back home.

Then Jett and Kenzie leaped from the sidewalk on Clancy's property, onto the public sidewalk. They jumped up and down, waving and screaming, "Avery! Avery!" A moment later, they tore down the sidewalk toward her. "We were afraid you weren't coming," Kenzie said, throwing herself at Avery's knees.

"We was!" Jett concurred.

Kenzie had a iron grip on Avery's knees, which made her wobble precariously.

"Daddy said he was ticked at you and you might not come to 'sketti dinner," Kenzie went on. "We think ticked means mad. Why is Daddy mad at you, Avery?"

"Yeah," Jett said, grabbing her knees, as well. "Why?"

Avery wobbled again, thinking quickly. She couldn't really tell them he was ticked because she'd asked a question about their mother, but what else *could* she say on short notice that would sort of be the truth?

While ideas ran through her head, she heard sniffles from down near her knees. She looked down and both Jett and Kenzie had tears streaming down their cheeks. "Don't cry," she pleaded.

"We're sad that Daddy's mad at you," Kenzie said between sobs.

Jett nodded his agreement. "We gots to cwy. We love you, Avery. We want you to come to 'sketti dinner."

"I was on my way to your house," she said in a failed attempt to make them stop crying.

"Yeah, but Daddy's ticked at you," Kenzie said. "If he's mad at you, why would you want to be around him?"

Avery remembered what he'd done to her in her bed, but she couldn't very well respond to Kenzie's question about that. "If you love someone," she said, "even if they're mad at you, you forgive them and move on."

"You do?" Kenzie asked, her little voice warbly.

"Yes. For instance, if Jett makes you mad, don't you forgive him because you love him?"

"I guess so." Kenzie looked at her brother. "Do you love me?"

He nodded, still crying.

"I love you, too, even when you make me mad."

"I love Daddy and Auntie Mo when they get mad at me." For whatever reason, Jett added, "Gwammy and

Gwampy never gets mad at me."

Kenzie hiccoughed and raised her head, trying to meet Avery eye-to-eye. "Daddy won't stay ticked at you, Avery. He loves you."

The two youngsters nodded and grasped her knees even tighter.

The next thing Avery knew, she went toppling backward.

Her head hit the sidewalk and everything went black.

"Dinner's ready!" Clancy called out. He put the salad on the table, then the bread, and stood back, trying to figure out what he'd forgotten. The spaghetti and meatballs had already been plated.

Then he remembered! Romano cheese. He went back to the fridge and grabbed it.

"Kids, dinner's ready!" he called out again. He stuck a spoon in the cheese container, then went looking for Kenzie and Jett.

They weren't in their rooms, nor were they anywhere in the house. When he approached the front door, he noticed it was open about half an inch. "Dammit to hell!" he muttered, flinging it open all the way.

"Kenzie! Jett!"

No answer. Clancy was alternately furious and concerned. They *knew* they weren't supposed to leave the yard, and their coats were hanging up in the mudroom. What the devil had they been thinking?

He walked down the sidewalk and looked left. No kids. He looked right, and there they were, sprawled on top of Avery, poking her, and crying.

Clancy dashed down the sidewalk and plucked Jett up first, then Kenzie. "You two know you're not supposed to leave the yard."

"We were waiting for Avery!" Kenzie retorted. "It's 'sketti night, remember? She loves 'sketti."

Jett contributed, "We saw hewa and we wan to meet hewa."

Clancy put the kids on their feet and stood with his hands on his hips and his feet planted apart, like he was some kind of human monolith. He glanced down at Avery. "What's wrong with her?"

The sobs down lower increased in intensity. "We didn't mean to make her fall," Kenzie said.

"We didn't," Jett agreed. "She falled backwawd and bonked hewa head."

Instantly concerned that she might be unconscious…or worse…Clancy squatted down beside the woman he loved and said, "Avery?" When he got no response, he brushed a finger against her cheek. Still no reaction. He placed a finger against her carotid artery to make sure she was still breathing. Thank God, she was. "You guys get back in the house."

"What about Avery?" Jett yelled.

"She's not mad at *you*, Daddy!" Kenzie informed him. "You're not gonna leave her out here, are you?"

"No," Clancy said. "Go back into the house. I'll carry her inside."

"Don't dwop hewa!" Jett said.

"I won't."

"Pwomise!" Jett said, planting his hands on his hips, just as his father had.

"I promise. Kenzie, run quick and make sure the door's still open."

His oldest child, still crying, spun around and ran as fast as she could down the icy sidewalk, then made a sharp left turn when she reached their sidewalk.

Jett streaked after her, though his strides weren't nearly as long.

Clancy lifted Avery off the cold concrete, being careful not to hurt her.

Her eyelids fluttered open just as he reached his front porch. "Where am I?"

"The kids knocked you to the ground and you hit your head on the sidewalk."

"Kids?"

"Kenzie and Jett."

She eyelids fluttered closed again.

"I'm so sorry, Avery."

She surprised him by asking, "For what?"

"For walking out on you earlier."

"Shit happens."

Surprised because he'd never heard her use a profanity before, he attempted to force a grin, but didn't quite make it. "Are we having our first argument?"

Her brow wrinkled, but she never opened her eyes. "I don't argue, but apparently, you do."

He grunted. "I guess I do, and again, I'm sorry."

"My head hurts," she said as he laid her on his bed.

"I'm going to lift you a little, so I can see if there's a bump." He felt her head with gentle fingers. "You've got a big egg on the back of your head."

"Too bad it's not Easter."

For a moment, he didn't get her humor, not that it was all that funny, anyway. He eased her back against the pillow.

Her eyes opened to slits. "Who are you?" she asked, genuinely puzzled.

"Clancy."

"What's wrong with her, Daddy?"

"I think she has a concussion."

"What's that?" Jett asked.

Clancy thought a moment for an answer his son could understand. "Her brain has been knocked for a loop."

Jett glanced at his sister with a stricken expression. "We killed Avery."

"She's not dead," Kenzie assured him, and climbed up on the bed to study Avery. "She's still breathing, isn't she, Daddy?"

Before Clancy could answer, his sister appeared in the bedroom doorway.

"What happened to Avery?" Mo asked.

Clancy explained the situation.

"Does she need to go to the ER?"

"Probably." He glanced at Avery, then back to his sister with a worried expression. "She asked me who I was."

Mo shook her head with disgust. "That's a sure sign of a concussion. Should we call an ambulance?"

"I'm pretty sure Avery wouldn't approve of that."

"Avery looks to be unconscious."

"Well, yeah, but…."

"Oh, for God's sake, Clancy. Put her in your SUV and I'll drive you."

"What about the kids?"

Mo shook her head. "They'll come with us," she said, speaking slowly, as if he could no longer understand English.

"Dinner's on the table," he said inanely.

"So I noticed when I reached the kitchen. I'll bring them back and feed them."

"What will I be doing?" he asked.

"Staying with Avery while she's being examined."

Of course, he would. What the hell was wrong with him?

CHAPTER 20

An Evening at the ER

It took Mo twelve minutes to reach the ER at Creekside Community Hospital.

Clancy carried Avery into the waiting room. When the receptionist noted she was unconscious, she pressed a button and a nurse, whose nametag read LUCY MORGAN, RN, ran into the lobby.

"What's wrong with her?" she asked.

"She fell and hit her head. She doesn't recognize me."

"I don't recognize you, either," the nurse said, falling short in the humor department. "Follow me."

Clancy did as instructed, trailing Nurse Morgan into the bowels of the ER.

"Room 103 is available."

"Which side of the hall will that be on?"

"Right side, third door down."

Clancy counted the doors, but when he got to Room 103, the gurney inside was already occupied.

"Darn!" the nurse said, hustling down the hall to the next room, and then the next one. "This one," she said, jab-pointing, as if Clancy were an idiot.

He entered the empty treatment room and laid Avery gently on the gurney.

Her eyelids fluttered, but she didn't open her eyes.

"You need to go back up front and give them your information."

"I don't have any information."

The nurse looked at him as if he'd lost his marbles. "Isn't this your wife?"

"No, she's a neighbor. She lives around the corner from us."

"Does she have insurance?"

"I have no idea. I never asked her."

The nurse frowned.

"I'll pay the bill, if she doesn't have insurance."

"You can let them know that at the front counter."

"I want to stay with Avery."

"You can come back when you're done checking her in," she said, as if talking to Jett.

Clancy wasn't sure he believed the nurse.

She took his indecision in her own hands, grabbing his arm to escort him back to the lobby.

"Name please?" the receptionist asked.

"Mine or the woman I brought in?" he asked.

The woman sighed. Her tone and her expression indicated she bordered on being irritated. "Both, please."

"Clancy O'Rourke and Avery Lark."

"Birth date."

"Sorry, I don't know her birth date."

"Address?"

He at least knew that, and her phone number.

"Insurance?"

"If she doesn't have insurance, I'll pay the bill," he said.

That earned him an incredulous stare and a curt nod.

"Can I go back now?"

"Not yet. Why did you bring her in today?"

"She fell on the sidewalk outside our house. I think she may have a concussion."

The receptionist narrowed her eyes on him. "You're a doctor now?"

"No, but she didn't recognize me. Isn't that a sign of concussion?"

"Possibly."

Clancy resisted the urge to reach over the counter to strangle her.

"Medications?"

"I don't know."

"Is she pregnant?"

Clancy stalled on that one. "I have no idea."

The receptionist eyed him in a way that told him she suspected he and Avery had some kind of intimate relationship going on.

"Are we done here?"

"Almost. I need your signature. Read this, then sign there." She nodded toward the rectangle on the counter.

He looked at the form, but nothing registered. Was he signing away his life, and possibly his kids' inheritance? At this point, did he even care? He signed with the non-pencil on the mechanical screen, then made a dash for the door leading back to the treatment rooms.

When he reached Room 107, Avery and the gurney were both gone. He asked the nearest body, which happened to be a Nurse's Aide, "Where have they taken her?"

She reached for the chart hanging outside the door. "To X-ray. They should be back shortly."

Thirty minutes later, Clancy was still pacing the hall outside Room 107. How long was *shortly*, anyway?

Ten more minutes passed and he spotted an ER doc. "What's taking so long?"

The doctor, who's name badge read SHARILYNN HORNBUCKLE, MD, glanced at the chart in the wall holder. "I'm sorry, but this isn't my patient."

Clancy went for broke, offering her a smile. "Would you mind checking for me? I was told she'd be back shortly, and that was forty-five minutes ago."

The doctor smiled back, but to Clancy, it didn't look friendly. "We're slammed right now and we only have two doctors and two nurses working today." She added, "Flu bug going around, you know."

He didn't, but he nodded, regardless, like that would move things along. He felt like a bobble-head dog on the dashboard.

The doctor sighed and reached for the chart.

Clancy knew damned good and well that no one had lifted that chart off the wall since the Nurse's Aide had done it earlier.

The doctor looked at him. "They might have seen something on the X-ray that necessitated a CT scan."

That shocked him. "Like what?"

"A hematoma, perhaps." She replaced the chart. "If you'll excuse me, I need to scrub for an emergency appendectomy."

Clancy backed up against the wall, thinking.

A possible hematoma?

That didn't sound good.

Not good at all.

Avery knew she was in a hospital, because she recognized the X-ray equipment in the room. She hadn't liked hospitals since she'd had her tonsils out when she was twelve.

Seventeen years ago, she'd hated the anesthetic, she'd hated the smell of the place, and her throat had been sore for almost two weeks after the tonsillectomy. A girl who loved burgers could only eat so much soft food after a surgery like that. Talk about agony!

"Ah, I see you're awake."

Her head still hurt like crazy, but she let her eyes wander the room, looking for the body that belonged to the voice. "What happened?"

"I heard you took a tumble on a sidewalk, and the lump on the back of your head verifies that."

"How long have I been here?"

"Um, almost an hour. There were others ahead of you today."

"Others?"

A soft chuckle preceded the response. "Yep. Among them was a toddler who swallowed two marbles. We X-rayed him to make sure they didn't go into his lungs, instead of his tummy."

"He's okay?"

"He'll be pooping them out any day now." The X-ray tech came out from behind the protection shield. "I want you to hold really still, okay? If you move, I'll have to take the shot again."

"Where's the man who brought me in?"

"Rumor has it, he's wearing out the floor in front of your treatment room."

"He should be. It's his fault I'm here." Why couldn't she recall his name?

"That sounds like an interesting story. Now, hold still." The X-ray tech moved behind the protective screen again. "Take a deep breath and hold it until I say breathe."

Avery sucked in a deep breath and held it. When she heard *breathe*, she blew it out.

"One more and we're done."

"Do I have a concussion?"

"I'm only the X-ray technician. I'm not supposed to comment on medical complaints."

"I take it that means I do."

The woman's head bobbed out from behind the screen. A huge grin split her face. "Turn your head slightly to the left, please." She disappeared again, then said, "Perfect. Another deep breath."

Once she'd finished, Avery said, "I have to pee."

"I'm calling the nurse now. Can you hold it until she comes for you?"

Avery would have nodded, but her head hurt like crazy. Instead, she whispered, "If I have to."

The nurse charged in a few minutes later. "Back to your room."

"I have to pee."

"There's a bathroom close-by. I'll help you when we get there."

Ten minutes later, Avery was back in her room. "Where's the man who brought me in?"

"I think he went to get a soft drink from the Coke machine."

"I'm thirsty. May I have some water, please?"

"I'll get you some. Would you like some warm blankets, too?"

Since she was chilled, Avery said, "That would be great."

Seconds later, Avery was alone, trying to get her brain to work.

The nurse returned with a cup filled with ice water, advising, "Take small sips." She spread the two warm blankets over Avery. "Rest now. It'll be at least half an hour before the doc gets to you."

"Thank you."

She took three small sips and set the cup down on the tray table. Just like that, the man's name came to her. He was Clancy O'Rourke. He had two adorable children, Jett and Kenzie. He was also the man she loved.

And then, there he was, standing in the doorway of her treatment room.

She held out her hand to him. "Come kiss me."

"Does that mean you remember who I am?"

"Yes. Close the door, too."

His eyes widened slightly, as if he had received an unspoken message. "I probably shouldn't."

"You probably should."

His eyes flared. He stepped inside and closed the door, advancing on her like some kind of sexy jungle cat. "You're injured, Avery, and this is an ER. You never know when someone's going to barge in."

"You can still kiss me."

He shook his head. "I think that fall did more than scramble your brain, love." He looked over his shoulder at the closed door. "I shouldn't."

"But you want to."

"I'll never get tired of kissing you."

"The nurse said the ER doc won't be in for thirty minutes. We have time."

He nodded and set his drink on the tray table alongside her water cup. Then he leaned down and gave her a gentle kiss, his hand on top of the warm blankets. "Did they remove all your clothes?"

"Everything except my panties and bra." She slow-blinked at him. "Even though I couldn't remember your name at first, I knew I loved you, Clancy."

"I'm glad you didn't forget that." He put his mouth back on hers and his kiss became less gentle and more passionate.

Minutes later, she said, "I'm sorry I can't put my arms around you."

Clancy shot her a rueful grin. "I can live with just a kiss for now" —he winked at her— "but later, ooh-la-la."

"I had no idea you could speak French," she murmured, just as the door swung open.

CHAPTER 21

CHECKING OUT OF THE ER

Dr. Pindter entered the room slowly, eyeing the two of them, as if he expected they'd been doing something they shouldn't be doing in a hospital ER. "How are you feeling?" he asked Avery.

"Drowsy," Avery answered honestly. "What do the X-rays show?"

"No hematoma," he said right off the bat, "but you do have a concussion." He glanced at Clancy, then back at Avery. "I'd like to send you home. Do you have anyone there to keep an eye on you for the next twenty-four hours?"

"No."

He sighed. "Then I suppose we'll have to get you a room upstairs."

"She can come to my place," Clancy said a little too quickly. "I can work from home tomorrow, and even the next day, if need be."

The doctor nodded, as if considering that option. His head swiveled back to Avery. "What are your thoughts?"

"I have a dog. As long as Clancy doesn't mind having

him as a house guest, I suppose that would work." She deliberately didn't make eye contact with Clancy.

"What kind of dog is it?" the doctor asked.

"A golden retriever. His tame is Twinkle, but Clancy's kids call him Twink."

"Cute name. I have a golden myself. They're great dogs."

"They sure are."

Dr. Pindter glanced at Clancy again. "Are you up for checking on Ms. Lark throughout the night?"

"Absolutely."

"You'll need to check her pupils. If one turns up larger than the other, you need to bring her right back here."

"Okay."

"She should stay away from rich foods for a few days. Maybe stick to a milkshake midday."

"That's doable. I can send my sister to DQ with the kids and they can bring back a shake."

The doctor nodded. "She shouldn't get too excited, and by that, I mean she should rest in bed for the next few days." He stared hard at Clancy, as if trying to make a point.

"No problem," Clancy said.

"Have her see her regular doctor for a checkup in a week." He looked at Avery then. "You do have a PCP, I presume?"

"Kevin Hornbuckle," Avery said.

"Ah, he's married to one of our ER docs, Sharilynn."

"I didn't know that."

"At any rate, you'll be in good hands with Kevin."

She didn't bother to tell Dr. Pindter that she hadn't seen Dr. Hornbuckle for over two years. "When can I leave?"

The doctor looked at his watch. "At seven."

Avery and Clancy both glanced at the wall clock. Forty minutes.

She looked at him.

He looked down at her. "I'll call Mo and have her get the spare bedroom ready."

"Okay." Considering the spare room was already ready, that would be a good trick.

The door opened. "Time to get you ready to go home," Nurse Morgan said. "Out you go, Clancy. Why don't you track down a wheelchair while I help Avery get back into her clothes?"

"I'd better call Mo to come get us," he said.

"Good idea," Avery agreed.

They stared at each other for a few seconds, then Clancy headed out the door.

Twenty minutes later, Avery was loaded into his SUV and he climbed in behind the wheel. "Do you want to swing through DQ now for a milkshake?"

"That sounds good," she said, wishing it didn't hurt to move her head. "I was really looking forward to 'sketti and meatballs, though."

"Ever eat cold spaghetti?"

"No."

"After I get you situated in bed, I'll make a plate. We can share it."

"The doc said no rich foods. I'll drink my milkshake and watch you eat, instead."

He pulled into the DQ drive-thru and drove up to the order screen. "What kind and how big?"

"A large strawberry, no whipped cream."

He looked over his shoulder. "What about you guys?"

"We'll have two small strawberries and one medium strawberry," Mo said. "And a medium fry."

"Do you all want whipped cream on your shakes?"

"No!" the replied in unison.

He gave the order, then drove forward to pay. A moment later, the person at the window handed over the drinks and the fries.

Avery took a tentative sip of her strawberry shake.

Clancy's eyes lowered to watch her suck on the straw.

Avery noticed and smiled at him.

"Do you need me to spend the night?" Mo asked when they reached his neighborhood.

"I can probably handle things on my own," Clancy said.

"I'm sure you can," Mo said in a wry tone, "but that's not what I asked."

Avery intervened, hoping to quell a sibling back-and-forth. "Can we stop by my place first? I need to get a few things."

"Sure." Clancy turned into the subdivision and made his way to her house. "I'll come in with you."

"That will be helpful."

As they walked slowly to her front door, he asked, "Am I forgiven for walking out on you earlier?"

"I forgave you for that hours ago."

"You did?"

"You sound surprised."

"It's left over from Mindy. She held a grudge for months when she didn't get her way."

"I don't hold grudges. They're useless."

"Good to know." He stopped long enough to kiss her.

"Does Avery taste like stwabewwies?" Jett called out from the open window of the SUV.

CHAPTER 22

RECUPERATING AT CLANCY'S

Breathless from his kiss, Avery dug her key out of her pocket and handed it to Clancy. "Why don't you go on ahead and unlock the door?"

Clancy frowned. "I shouldn't leave you. What if you fall?"

"I promise, I won't."

The frown remained on his face.

"Once the door's unlocked, you can come back and get me, if I'm not already there by then."

He shook his head at her convoluted response. "Life with you is going to be interesting."

She blinked up at him and smiled. "Let Twink out before you come back to get me."

It was obvious he didn't like that idea, but he hustled away. The outside lights flashed on, lighting his way. He returned two minutes later, scooped her up in his arms, and kissed her again. "I love you."

She smiled again and offered him a taste of her milkshake.

Not one to turn down an offer to put his lips where

hers had just been, he took a sip.

"I can walk, you know."

He smiled down at her. "I like having you in my arms, and besides, the walkway is icy."

"Ah."

Her carried her inside and kicked the door shut.

"Bedroom first," she said.

He strode down the hall, directly to her bedroom, where he set her on the bed. "Tell me what you need and I'll grab it."

Avery thought a minute. "My polar bear PJs out of the second drawer, and some fresh underwear out of the top drawer. Enough for two or three days."

He went to do her bidding. "Where's your overnight bag?"

"In the closet, top shelf. I also have a small go-bag in the bathroom. It has sundries in it, so I'll need that, too."

"Anything from the closet?"

"A clean pair of jeans and a sweatshirt ought to do me."

He nodded, and once everything was packed, he ran the overnight bag out to the SUV. When he came back, he said, "The troops are getting restless. Are you ready?"

"As I'll ever be." She pushed up off the bed. "This time, I'll walk. You can make sure I don't fall flat on my face." She took one step and cried, "Wait!"

He jerked, startled. "What?"

"We need to get Twinkle and his food, too."

"I'll get you in the SUV, then come back for him." He held out his hand. "Your key, please."

Avery dug into her pocket for it, then realized Clancy had never given it back. "You still have it."

He rammed his hand into his jacket pocket and gri-maced. "So I do."

"Twink's going to love seeing Kenzie and Jett."

"They'll love having him at the house."

Ten minutes later, Mo unlocked Clancy's front door. Twinkle followed Kenzie and Jett into the house and Clancy carried Avery in. She'd fallen asleep before the SUV had backed out of her driveway.

Mo helped carry in her stuff and followed Clancy down the hallway. "Stop, Clancy!"

"What?"

"The doc said she shouldn't have any excitement, right?"

"Right."

"So, back up and put her in the spare bedroom."

"Mo—"

"Don't Mo me, big brother, or I'll sic the dog on you."

Clancy looked down at Twinkle and grinned.

Twink gave him a doggie grin back.

A little after midnight, Clancy left the easy chair in the spare bedroom and climbed into bed with Avery.

At seven-thirty, she began to stir. At seven-forty-five, she opened her eyes and smiled at him.

"How do you feel?"

"Better than I did last night, but my head still hurts some."

"The doc said you can take ibuprofen."

"After I eat something, I will." She raised a hand and stroked his cheek. "I love you."

"I love you, too. Does that mean you'll marry me?"

"Don't spoil the moment, Clancy."

He raised up on his elbow and stared down at her. "Why are you so reluctant to talk about marriage?"

Her gaze darted away, then came back to meet his. "Honestly? I don't know. Maybe it's because we've only known each other a short time."

"People fall instantly in love all the time, Avery. It just

so happens, we're in that category. When you're in love, you should tie the knot." When she didn't speak, he continued. "As I mentioned before, if we were married, we wouldn't have to do all this sneaking around."

Avery silently acknowledged that sneaking around did cause a few problems.

"I want to wake up every morning with you next to me," Clancy said, fingering her nipple. "I want to eat my meals with you every day. I want to make love to you whenever I want to."

"You want a lot of things."

"Don't you?"

"Well…yes, but that doesn't mean I'm going to get them."

His finger went to her chin and gently forced her to look at him. "Don't you think we'll be compatible?"

She offered him a wry smile. "I'm pretty sure we won't have any problems that way."

"Then give me another reason besides we-haven't-known-each-other-that-long."

Avery hardly ever cried, so she was surprised when her eyes filled with tears. "I don't have another reason."

"Don't cry, love."

"I can't help it, I—"

He stopped her with a kiss.

When he pulled away, she continued. "I love you, I love your kids, I want your babies."

He kissed her again.

"But there are so many issues related to marriage."

"Like what?" he pressed. "Name one."

She hesitated, then asked, "Where would we live?"

"Not your house. Lovely though it is, it's too small for a growing family."

"Your house won't do when the babies start coming, either."

"How many babies?" he asked, as if he'd never really

thought about numbers.

"Two or three, or maybe even four."

He frowned. "We could add on, since my lot is fairly large, or we could buy a bigger house on a bigger lot." He swallowed. "Four more kids?"

"You like kids, don't you?"

"Well, yeah, but four more?"

"It's an estimate, Clancy, not a given."

"You have a dog, too."

"True."

He thought for a moment, then said, "I guess four more kids would be okay. What else?"

"My work. I love writing game apps, but with six kids running around the house, how would I manage it?"

"Unless you had quadruplets, wouldn't they come in stages?"

"Quadruplets? Heaven forbid!"

He grinned with a shrug. "If work is that important to you, we'll figure something out."

"Why does that sentence have a question mark at the end of it?"

"Did it?"

"Yes."

"Hunh." He thought further. "How much does your business bring in every year?"

"Last year, I grossed one-sixty."

"A hundred and sixty thousand dollars?" he asked, amazed and more than a little shocked.

"Yes. Plenty of people pay for extras on all my games, you know."

"No, I didn't know. In fact, I never thought to ask which games you'd written."

She named off the twelve best sellers.

"Holy crap, Avery. I play two of those games."

"Hooray for you."

"Don't go getting snarky on me."

"Sorry, I never thought…never mind."

"You never thought what?"

"That you were a guy who played game apps."

"I'm thirty-four, love. I grew up playing games, and there's a few I still enjoy when I want to relax."

"I write them and I never play them," she admitted. "For me, the creativity of writing the game is the challenge."

"I get that," he said. "Creativity is the mainstay of my business, too."

"Exactly what *is* your business?"

"Promotional products. We can supply anything from matchbooks to travel trailers, all with your business logo on them."

"Wow. That's a broad scope of items."

"I know, and it keeps me busy."

She sighed. "See, we hardly know anything about each other."

"Isn't the fun in learning?"

"Don't get all academic on me."

He grinned.

"Being so busy, does that mean you won't be able to make love when you want to?"

"There are work hours and there are making-love hours, and never the twain shall meet."

"I had no idea you could wax poetic."

"Is that a problem?"

"Not for me."

"Good to know."

"Do you still want to know all the reasons why I'm resisting saying yes to your marriage proposal?"

"Are there more aside from the ubiquitous *because*?" he asked, slightly incredulous. He slid his hand over her belly, fingering her bellybutton.

"There might be, but how am I supposed to think when you're touching me…."

CHAPTER 23

THE DAY AFTER THE ER

Kenzie put her finger up to her lips and said, "Shhh," to her brother.

"Why do I gots to be quiet, Kenzie? Isn't it time for Avery to wake up?"

"Daddy had to take her to the hospital yesterday, Jett. She needs her rest. Remember, we knocked her down and she hit her head?"

That observation got both of them teary-eyed.

"We didn't mean to huwt hewa," Jett whispered.

"I know, but we did. Daddy said she needs sleep now, more than anything."

"Okay, but when will she wake up?"

"When her eyes are open, she'll be awake."

"She's gonna miss bweakfast."

"She can eat later."

"Okay, you two," Clancy said, approaching them from behind. "Didn't I tell you to leave Avery alone?"

"She gots to eat," Jett protested.

"If she's hungry when she wakes up, we'll give her some 'sketti and meatballs," Kenzie informed him.

"Or something else," Clancy inserted. "Now the two of you hightail it to the kitchen. You have twenty minutes to eat before you leave."

They scurried away, but Clancy remained behind, watching Avery sleep.

He pulled her door closed and leaned against it, ordering a certain part of his body to settle down.

Minutes later, he returned to the kitchen, where Mo had served the kids one of their favorite breakfasts, Corn Pops in blueberry yogurt.

The three of them looked him up-and-down, which reminded him that he had on jeans and a sweatshirt, not a suit. He also thanked God that his hard-on had gone soft.

Kenzie took a bite of her cereal, then asked, "Are you staying home today, Daddy?"

"Yes. Since Avery has a concussion, the doctor said she needs watching for twenty-four hours. I can work here and watch her at the same time."

"What about us?" Jett asked.

"Kenzie has school today and you have pre-school. Mo will pick you up afterward. The two of you will go for lunch anywhere you want and after she picks up Kenzie, you'll go for an ice cream at Dingy's. When you get home after that, I expect you both to be as quiet as possible."

"Why?" Jett asked.

"Remember when you fell on the steps?"

He nodded.

"Remember the bump you got on your forehead?"

Again, Jett nodded.

"Well, Avery has a bump on the back of her head that's four times bigger than your bump."

"Is fowa times biggew weally big, Daddy?"

"It weally is, Jett." Clancy rolled his eyes for mimicking a toddler. "Are we agreed?"

The kids nodded solemnly, then turned their full attention back to breakfast.

"A word, Clancy?" Mo signaled they should leave the kitchen.

Before they reached the door, Jett asked, "What about Twink, Daddy? He'll get lonely without us hewa."

"Twink will be fine, Jett. I'll put him outside so he can chase squirrels."

Jett giggled. "He won't catch 'em."

"No, he won't, but that won't stop him from trying."

"Does Twink like the snow?"

"Avery said he does, and before you ask, I won't leave him outside too long while it's snowing."

"You'd better not," Kenzie said. "We don't want him to freeze."

Jett nodded his agreement.

Clancy followed Mo down the hall. "What's up?"

"Is Avery going to be all right?"

"The ER doc said she will, if she rests like he told her to."

Mo's eyes darted here, there, and everywhere before they landed on him again. "I'm worried about her."

"So am I."

"Are you really?"

"Of course. Why are you questioning that?"

"The kids said they heard moans and groans coming from her room last night." She sighed. "I can only assume that means neither one of you was sleeping."

"MYOB, Mo."

"I am minding my own business, Clancy, and right now, I'm worried about Avery. If she's recovering from a concussion, should she really be having nonstop sex with you?"

"What's sex, Daddy?" Jett asked.

"Yeah, Daddy," Kenzie chimed in. "What's sex?"

Clancy looked down, surprised to find both kids standing beside him and Mo. He glanced back at his sister. "Now you've done it."

Mo looked down and said, "Get back to the kitchen right now and finish your cereal!" She pointed her finger to make sure they knew she was serious.

They turned and scampered back to the kitchen.

"*I've* done it?" she shot back. "You're the one who's having sex with her."

"FYI, we weren't having sex, and I didn't bring it up in the first place. It's your fault the kids heard the word *sex*!"

She gaped at him. "You're impossible, and don't bother trying to explain what those moans and groans were, either!"

"I may be impossible, but you're incorrigible. Start thinking about how you're going to explain what sex is to a three-year-old and a five-year-old."

Mo stomped her foot, as if she were five. "I already know what I'm going to say, Clancy. So there."

"Do tell," he shot back.

"I'm going to explain that some people call kissing sex and leave it at that. If I make a bigger issue out of it, that'll be your problem, not mine." On that slightly snide note, she headed down the hall, leaving her brother speechless.

Avery woke with the sun shining in her right eye. She wasn't ready to greet the day, but apparently, the sun thought she was.

She rolled over, intent on finding another position that didn't involve the sun hitting her face and encountered Clancy's big body.

That stumped her, because he should be at work, not sound asleep next to her in the spare bedroom

She considered waking him up, then decided he probably hadn't gotten enough sleep last night, busy as he'd been "taking care" of her.

As quietly as she could, she slid out of the bed and headed for the bathroom. She felt a little dizzy, so she decided to forego a shower. She used the facilities, washed her hands and face, and brushed her teeth. After that, she went back to the spare bedroom. She debated closing the door, and decided instead to pull it almost closed. She headed down the hallway to the kitchen, where she opened the fridge.

There, on the second shelf, was the leftover 'sketti from the night before. Next to it sat a bowl with one meatball. Avery had never eaten cold pasta, but Clancy swore it was delicious. Still being quiet, she dished up a mound of 'sketti into the meatball bowl.

Tempting as it was to put the bowl in the microwave, she decided not to. Sound traveled and she didn't want to wake Clancy.

She recovered the spaghetti and returned the bowl to the fridge. She grabbed a fork and a napkin and headed to the living room with her breakfast. The remote was on the coffee table. She hit the right buttons to turn on the TV and punched in the channel numbers for TCM, which played many of her old black-and-white favorites. Moments later, she sat down on the floor about five feet in front of the TV so she could hear it.

When Clancy found her there almost half an hour later, she had the partially eaten meatball on the end of her fork, nibbling it. Tears dribbled down her cheeks.

She barely noticed when he sank down beside her. "Why are you crying, love?"

"William Holden just died and his lover, Jennifer Jones, is wondering how she'll spend the rest of her life without him."

Clancy glanced at the TV. "What movie is this?"

"*Love is a Many Splendored Thing*." She sniffled. "It's so sad."

"Then why are you watching it?"

She turned to look at him. "It's one of my favorite old movies, Clancy. It's romantic. She's widowed, and he's married, and they fall in love."

Clancy shook his head. "You and my mom are going to get along great. She loves old movies, too."

Avery took a bite of the meatball. "I'd love to meet her someday."

"I'll introduce you as soon as you recover."

She deliberately batted her eyelashes at him. "I think I'm fully recovered already, don't you?"

"I mean from the bump on your head."

"That, too."

He shook his head again. "What am I going to do with you?"

"I can think of several things." She put the meatball back in the bowl and set it aside.

"Did you like eating cold pasta?"

She nodded. "It was delicious."

He stared at her in stunned surprised when she started unbuttoning her pajama top. He stood and extended his hand to her.

"What's wrong with right here?"

"Nothing," he said. He pulled back his hand and started unbuttoning his shirt.

Her eyes traveled down his impressive form and landed on his zipper. "I see you're ready."

"Where you're concerned, Avery, I'm always ready."

CHAPTER 24

AFTER MAKING LOVE

For the second time that day, Avery awoke in the spare bedroom.

If only Clancy were in the bed with her, it might have been a perfect day, despite the ache in her head, and the bump on the back of it.

She threw back the covers, surprised to find she was completely naked. Had she not heard the vague sounds of kids' voices wafting down the hall, she might have skipped putting her PJs on.

Feeling like a woman well-loved, she pulled on the bottoms, then her top and buttoned it. She opened the bedroom door, surprised to find Kenzie and Jett sitting on the floor in the hallway.

"She's awake!" Jett screamed, grabbing her legs.

Avery wobbled and reached for the door frame to steady herself.

"Jett, you're gonna make Avery fall again. Let go of her legs!" Kenzie ordered.

Her brother complied immediately. "Sowwy, Avery! I'm just excited 'cuz you woke up. Finally! We been sitting hewa for a weally long time, waiting."

Avery smiled down at him and decided to join them on the floor. "How was school and pre-school today?"

"I got to read out loud," Kenzie said. "I only stumbled over one word."

"Which word was that?" Avery asked.

"Trampoline."

"That's a big word for a kindergartner."

"Miss Graham said I did a good job of sounding it out."

Avery reached over and hugged her, which made Kenzie smile. "How about you, Jett?"

"We had show-and-tell today. I told evewyone how Kenzie and I made you fall, and you had to go to the hospital, and now yowa staying at ouwa house so Daddy can keep an eye on you." He frowned. "I told them when you feel betta, you'll come with me to show, 'cuz it is *show* and tell."

Avery grinned and hugged him, too. "I can do that."

Jett grinned back. "I love you, Avery."

"I love you, too, Jett, and you, too, Kenzie."

"This looks like a happy group," Clancy said, creeping up on them. "Wouldn't you all be more comfortable sitting in chairs?"

Avery glanced up and smiled. "I don't think so, Clancy. There's something about being on the floor that's just…amazing."

His eyes flared, leaving no doubt that he got her message loud and clear—she'd enjoyed every minute they'd spent on the living room floor, making love.

"I ordered two pizzas for dinner."

"What kind, Daddy?" Kenzie asked.

"One half-pepperoni, half-cheese, and the other is a combo with no onions."

Avery was impressed that he remembered she didn't like onions on her pizza. "Sounds yummy."

"It will be," he promised, which told her he wasn't talking about pizza. "Go wash your hands, kids, and let me know when the pizza guy shows up."

Neither Kenzie nor Jett moved.

Clancy looked down at them and said, "Did you hear what I said?"

"Yeah," Kenzie said, "but we want to talk to Avery. Can't you wait for the pizza guy?"

"Tell you what," Avery intervened. "Go wash your hands and we'll meet you in the living room. We can all be together while we're waiting for the pizza guy."

Kenzie and Jett exchanged a look, then got to their feet and dashed off to the bathroom.

Clancy held out his hand to Avery. "You're a terrific mediator."

She smiled as he pulled her up. "Mom taught me mediating logistics when my brothers' argued as teenagers."

"Your brothers argued?" he asked, feigning shock.

"Regularly." She grinned. "Usually over a girl, but sometimes over other things."

Clancy pulled her tight to his body. "Imagine that. Fighting over a girl." Before she could respond, he kissed her.

"Daddy, since you and Avery have a lot of sex, does that mean she's gonna marry you?" Kenzie asked from the bathroom doorway.

Clancy and Avery pulled away from each other.

Clancy said, "Not necessarily, Kenzie."

"What does she mean by sex?" Avery asked.

"You can thank Mo for that," Clancy said, scowling. "I'll explain later."

Avery wanted an explanation right then and there, but with two little kids staring at them with unbridled interest, she knew why it would have to wait. She took Clancy's hand and led him down the hall to the living room.

Kenzie and Jett trailed behind them, giggling all the way.

For some reason, Avery felt the need to distance herself from Clancy, mainly because of the *sex* comment. What the heck *had* Mo meant?

"Can we eat in the living room?" Kenzie asked after several moments of silence.

Clancy jerked his head in her direction. "There's no place to eat in here, Kenz."

"We could use the coffee table. That's what we do when Mo lets us eat in here."

"Mo lets you eat in the living room?" he asked, sounding a little confounded.

"Sure. She always tells us not to make a mess, because if we do, we have to clean it up."

"Mo's going to make a great mom," Avery said.

Clancy shook his head. "Okay, but Auntie Mo's rule goes for me, too. If you make a mess, you clean it up."

"We won't," Jett said, his little voice serious. "I don't like cleaning up messes."

The doorbell rang. Clancy went to answer and returned with two medium-size pizza boxes.

"Are we really going to eat all that?" Avery asked.

"We like cold pizza for breakfast around here," he informed her.

"I have to admit, I've never had cold pizza for breakfast, either, but I'm willing to give it a try."

"You'll love it," Kenzie said, clearing the coffee table. "I'll get the paper plates and napkins." She ran off toward the kitchen.

"I'll get some drinks," Clancy said, setting the two boxes on the coffee table. "What would you like, Avery?"

"I don't suppose I can have a beer?"

"The ER doc didn't say you couldn't. Sierra Nevada okay?"

She nodded.

"I'll have a woot beew, Daddy."

Clancy smiled at his son. "Want to help me?"

"Suwa!" Jett popped up off the floor and lunged at Clancy's legs.

His dad lifted him and said, "Be right back."

The pizza smelled so divine, Avery couldn't help opening one of the boxes for a quick peek. She snatched a piece of pepperoni, hoping no one would notice.

Kenzie returned with a spatula and the paper goods. "Good thing the coffee table is big," she noted.

"It sure is," Avery agreed.

"Do you love my daddy?"

Avery didn't hesitate. "Yes."

"He loves you, too, so why don't you get married?"

"I'm still considering his proposal."

"What's to consider? You love him, he loves you. Auntie Mo says love is what makes the world go 'round."

Out of the mouths of babes, and aunts. Avery nodded and said, "That's what I've heard, too."

Jett came racing back into the room with his root beer.

"When we eat in the living room," Kenzie said, "Jett has to have his drink in a plastic glass with a lid and a straw in it."

"Smart," Avery said, snatching another piece of pepperoni.

"I saw that," Clancy said. "No sneaking pepperoni slices until everyone is at the table."

Feeling a little perverse, Avery looked back at the open box and grabbed yet another piece of pepperoni. She looked directly at Clancy when she popped it into her mouth.

His eyes did that flare thing again. The one that always got her so excited.

CHAPTER 25

ANOTHER DAY IN PARADISE

Avery and Clancy made love for two solid hours, then they slept for an hour. When they woke again, they made love again.

And so it went throughout the night.

At six a.m., Clancy loomed over her. "I'm worried that I'm not letting you get enough rest."

"Do you hear me complaining?"

"No." He dipped his head, aiming for her breast. "I need to get more condoms."

Avery wished she'd bought a box herself, but what he was doing to her breasts felt so good, she decided not to mention it. An hour later, she murmured, "Isn't it time for the kids to get up?"

He nodded, though it was obvious he was more interested in caressing her body.

"What if I fix breakfast this morning?"

"I don't think so. You're supposed to be resting."

She laughed softly. "It's your fault I haven't been."

"I can't help it, Avery. I'm so gone for you, it's not even funny." He leaned over and tongued her nipple.

"Clancy?"

"Hmm?"

"I need to go home today."

He sighed. "I know."

Outside his bedroom door, Twink whined. From the whispers, the kids were up, too.

"What if we come to your house for dinner tonight? I'll order Italian from Amore, since they deliver."

"That sounds delicious, but I'm not sure I'll have all my decorating done by then."

"You're supposed to be resting, not decorating."

She grabbed his head and forced him to look at her. "Really?"

"I could help you."

"You could, but would we make any progress?"

"Probably not."

"What time would you arrive for dinner?"

"We could be there by five. The kids could play with Twink and watch TV, and you and I could sneak away for a quick wall-banger."

"Wall-banger?" she asked.

"You know, you wear a skirt and no panties. I lean you against a wall and hold you up. We have a wall-banger."

"Gee, that sounds oddly unfamiliar," she said, trying to keep her tone disingenuous.

He grinned. "I'm full of good ideas."

"You're full of something, all right."

"Will you marry me, Avery?"

"I'm still thinking about that."

He shook his head, looking sorrowful. "You're killing me, you know that?"

Clancy drove to the end of the block, turned right, and

right again, and pulled into Avery's driveway. "Stay put until I come around and open your door."

Avery smiled at him.

Clancy smiled back. "Maybe we can try out that wall-banger ahead of time."

She shook her head. "Is sex all you think about?"

"Only in relation to you. When I'm not thinking about sex, I think about you." His smile disappeared. "Don't you think about me?"

"All the time," she said.

"See? This is why we should get married."

She resorted to her original argument. "We've only known each other for a little over a month, Clancy."

"Did I ever tell you my parents only knew each other for two weeks when they tied the knot?"

"I believe you did. My parents only knew each other for six weeks before they got married."

His mouth literally dropped open. "You come from a family of people who marry after six weeks and you're still telling me no?"

"I didn't say no. I'm a thinker, and my parents were overcome with romantic bliss."

"Don't tell me you aren't overcome with romantic bliss."

"I won't, because I am, but I'm more practical than my parents."

"I've met your folks, remember? I'd say you're all equally practical."

"Maybe now, but when they were younger, all they could think about was sex, sex, sex."

"Did they tell you that?"

"Not in so many words, but I do have three siblings, you know, and we're all close together in age."

"I'm sensing an offspring pattern you neglected to mention."

"Sorry."

"Are any of them married?"

"No."

"So you'd be the first one."

"I guess I would."

"Is that the real reason you're vacillating?"

Was it? The more she thought about it, the more she realized he might be right. "Maybe."

"How old are your siblings?"

"Evie is twenty-seven, Drake is thirty-one, and Bent is thirty-three."

"I take it you're in that mix somewhere."

"I'm after Evie and before Drake."

"Which makes you somewhere between twenty-eight and thirty."

"Gosh," she said, eyeing him with wide eyes, "you're brilliant, especially given that I mentioned before that I'm twenty-nine."

He shook his head again. "One of the things I love about you is that you're a smart ass."

"Hee-haw."

He laughed.

"Let's go in and try out that wall-banger, shall we?"

Two hours later, Avery kissed Clancy goodbye at her front door.

He started down the walk, then turned and asked, "What should I order for dinner?"

"I love Amore's ravioli."

"Sounds good. Hope you make progress on your decorating."

"I will…and thanks for the wall-banger."

He grinned. "I aim to please." He climbed into his SUV and drove away, waving.

Avery closed and locked the door and headed straight

for her bedroom. No matter what she and Clancy did together, it was amazing.

She pulled her robe off and hung it on a hook in the closet. Later, she'd put on some nice clothes, but for decorating, she decided on jeans and an old tee shirt. First, though, a shower.

Once she was dressed, she decided to hang her new ornaments on the tree with the silver curly-cue hangers she'd bought. When she stood back to examine her handy work, she found herself completely enthralled with the multi-color twinkling lights *and* the ornaments. From here on out, she'd add an ornament every Christmas, and if she married Clancy and they had kids, their ornaments would go on the tree, too, along with Kenzie and Jett's.

Satisfied so far, she decided to put up the few pieces of wall décor next. She moved the wreath from the kitchen and hung it over the fireplace. The glittery silver moon went on the wall next to the tree. As for the other two pieces, one went in the dining room and the other in the kitchen, where the wreath had hung.

Next, the table décor. The angels went on the mantle and she placed the Snow Babies on the small table next to the sofa. And so it went.

At four-thirty, Avery wandered through her home, examining everything. Now, it felt like Christmas.

She hurried down the hall to her bedroom and opened the closet door. She'd bought a new red dress for Christmas. It had a beaded bodice and a flare skirt, which would be perfect for wall-banging, but not for tonight, since the kids would be there. She stripped and bypassed the strapless bra she'd bought at the same time, going instead for her black bra and briefs. After that, she pulled on black slacks and a magenta cowl-neck sweater. She examined herself in the mirror and decided the cowl neck was too much. She exchanged it for a button-front teal sweater, leaving the top two buttons undone.

She padded barefoot down the hall just as the doorbell rang.

She flung it open, startled that it was the delivery guy from Amore.

"Dinner delivery," he said. "You look mighty pretty ma'am." He handed over the big bag stuffed with boxes.

"Thank you." Behind him, Clancy, Kenzie, and Jett came up the walk.

The appreciation in Clancy's eyes made her day all worth it.

CHAPTER 26

KENZIE'S CHRISTMAS PROGRAM

Clancy called Avery at noon on Tuesday and invited her to the Christmas program at Kenzie's school.

"I'd love to come," Avery said, wondering why he'd waited so long to ask her.

"I'd love to have you come," Clancy replied in his sexiest voice.

"Clancy!"

"I can't help myself. You bring out the animal in me."

"I love the animal in you." Even though she already knew the particulars, because she'd been involved in making Kenzie's costume, she said, "Tell me more about Kenzie's Christmas program."

"It's Thursday night, at seven. It'll probably last an hour. I thought we could all go for an ice cream afterward, and after that, you and I can do you-know-what."

"That sounds like fun. Will you pick me up, or should I drive myself?"

Sounding a little shocked, he said, "This is a date, Avery. We'll pick you up at six-forty. Kenzie has to be there ten minutes early, because her class is on first."

"So I heard."

"Who told you?"

"Did Kenzie not tell you I made her costume?"

"No, she didn't." He sighed. "I knew she was keeping some kind of secret, but no matter what I tried, I couldn't worm it out of her."

"Well, it is a surprise."

"I don't like surprises."

"Too bad."

He grinned. "Not scared of me, huh?"

"Not scared of you at all, and don't go looking in Kenzie's room for her costume, because I have it."

"Why?"

"I had a few last-minute details to finish."

"Ah." He was silent for a moment, then said, "They're waving at me to hurry. We're having a lunch meeting in the conference room."

"You'd better go, then."

"I'm missing you like crazy, Avery."

"I miss you, too. See you Thursday night."

Avery made a small garment bag out of a pillow case to carry Kenzie's dress.

When Clancy knocked on her door, she gave him a chaste kiss, then pulled her door shut and locked it.

"Is that all I get?" he asked, eyeing her with his usual hunger.

"For now. Later, you get a lot more."

He reached for the garment bag.

Avery held it out of his reach. "No way, Clancy. I don't trust you not to peek."

"She's my kid," he said, making another grab for the bag.

"You'll spoil the surprise and Kenzie will be crushed."

He glanced at his SUV. Kenzie was staring at him with her mouth open, like she was screaming. He looked back at Avery. "Okay, I give, but I need another kiss to hold me."

She obliged and they walked to the SUV holding hands.

Once they reached the elementary school, he let Kenzie off at the front door. "Where are you going?" he asked Avery.

"I need to help Kenzie get into her costume. See you inside."

"Break a leg," he said to his daughter and drove off to find a parking spot.

"Why did Daddy say to break a leg?" Kenzie asked Avery.

"Break a leg is show business talk for good luck."

Kenzie smiled. "Daddy's really going to be surprised, isn't he?"

"He sure is, and Jett will be, too, unless you told him."

Kenzie shook her head vigorously. "If I told Jett, the whole neighborhood would know."

Avery grinned. "We'd better hurry, or they won't be able to start on time."

Avery made her way out of the stage area and looked for Clancy and Jett. As it happened, they were seated in the front row, next to Mo. Right behind them were the rest of Clancy's family. Mo made introductions, since Avery had yet to meet them.

At seven o'clock straight up, Kenzie's teacher, Miss Graham, ducked between the curtains. She wore a sparkly dress of red-and-green and waved at the audience. "Good evening, everyone! Thank you for coming to our annual holiday program...and bringing your Christmas spirit with you. Before my kindergarten class starts us off, I'd like to share a quick story with you. Kenzie O'Rourke is our lead singer. She proposed a suggestion to the class, and we all agreed. Our pianist agreed it would be perfect, too, and so…I present to you, *our* version of "Rudolph, the Red-Nosed Reindeer."

The curtain slid open, the lights dimmed, and the kindergarten class was revealed. All were dressed like Santa's reindeer, except for Kenzie, who stood quietly in the middle of the reindeer half-circle in her flowing red dress. She had a red ball on her nose and red antlers on her head.

The pianist began to play.

The reindeer began to clomp softly.

Kenzie activated the battery pack in the velvet pouch hanging from her waist. The mini-Christmas lights on her dress began to blink, and she began to sing. "You know Dasher and Dancer and Prancer and Vixen, Comet and Cupid and Donner and Blitzen, but do you recall the most famous reindeer of all?"

The audience laughed and broke into wild applause.

Clancy exchanged a stunned, but proud look with Avery. "Kenzie looks amazing."

"Aren't you glad you didn't know?"

He nodded and glanced back at the stage. It took him a minute to notice Jett had joined his sister's class. His son was doing a fair imitation of reindeer clomping.

Clancy reached for Avery's hand. "Did Miss Graham okay Jett joining the class?"

"I don't think so." Even though Jett was adorable being a reindeer, Avery worried he might be in trouble for barging in on the performance. "She is giving him a teacher look."

Clancy sighed. "I guess we'll find out after the show."

Avery nodded, hoping they were worried for nothing.

"Kenzie, the red-nosed reindeer, had a very shiny

nose, and if you ever saw it, you would even say it glows."

Clancy turned to her. "I love you, Avery."

She faced him with happy tears streaming down her cheeks. "I love you, too."

"Then one foggy Christmas Eve, Santa came to say, Kenzie, with your nose so bright, won't you guide my sleigh tonight? Then how the reindeer loved her, as they shouted out with glee. Kenzie, the red-nosed reindeer, you'll go down in history."

The pianist paused only briefly and the song began again. When the kindergartners finished, the audience rose, clapping and whistling like crazy.

All the reindeer, Miss Graham, Jett, and Kenzie, the red-nosed reindeer, took a bow. Kenzie's antlers tilted and fell off.

Jett grabbed them and positioned them on his head, laughing.

Calls for an encore came from the audience. Since the song was short, the pianist grinned and began to play again.

Kenzie waved to the audience, and sang, "You know Dasher and Dancer…."

Once the program was over, and before they could leave the small auditorium, Miss Graham approached the O'Rourke's, her eye on Jett.

He smiled up at her, which surely must have softened her heart.

"Did you have my permission to join the kindergarten class?"

"No, but Kenzie said I could."

"Oh, she did, did she?"

Jett nodded enthusiastically and glanced at his sister.

Kenzie folded her hands in front of her, looking a little prim and a little devilish. "I thought it was the least I could do, since I'd kept such a big secret from him. Jett doesn't like secrets."

"Neither do I," Miss Graham said. "However, I'll make an exception in this case." She bent down to look Jett directly in the eye. "I look forward to having you in my class in two years, Jett."

His smile broadened. "Thank you. I hope it'll still be fun by then."

"Oh, it will," Miss Graham promised with a wink.

Unexpectedly, Jett threw his arms around her neck. "Kenzie said yowa good spowt."

Miss Graham hugged him back. "You and your sister are good sports, too." She straightened and glanced at Clancy, then Avery. "You did a fabulous job on Kenzie's dress, Avery."

"Thank you, Derry. She helped me design it."

"Any time you want to help in the classroom, let me know. We can use expertise from someone with an imagination like yours."

"Sign me up," Avery said, "but not until after Christmas." She shot Clancy a look.

He stared back at her with those hungry eyes of his.

"Merry Christmas," Miss Graham said, and walked toward another group of parents.

The O'Rourke family had gathered in the parking lot, as if waiting for Clancy, Avery, and the kids to show up.

"Great concert," said Clancy's dad, Mike. The others agreed.

"Can you guys join us at Dingy's?" Clancy asked.

As if they'd expected to be asked, they glanced at Clancy, then at Avery.

Mo said, "We all have stuff to do, but thanks for the invitation."

The others nodded, but Avery was suspicious, especially because Mo's lame excuse was so vague.

"It's been a delight meeting you, Avery," Sally O'Rourke said. "I hope you'll join us for our annual Christmas party, a week from Saturday."

A little stunned, Avery nodded. "That would be lovely. Thank you."

Clancy's family bid their goodnights, headed to their separate vehicles, and drove away.

Avery, Clancy, Kenzie, and Jett made their way to Dingy's Ice Cream Parlor.

"What's the real reason they didn't want to join us?" Avery asked.

"They read the signs," Clancy said.

This time, she didn't bother to ask for an explanation.

The four of them entered the ice cream parlor. Kenzie still wore her red dress, but had removed her red nose, and Jett had the antlers on his head, though they were tilted.

Clancy ordered four strawberry sundaes, with whipped cream on top, while Avery and the kids found a table.

"You were amazing," Clancy said to Kenzie when he sat down with them.

"Avery gave me the idea," she said, smiling. "After I talked to my teacher and the class about it, Avery agreed to make me a red dress, with Christmas lights."

"She did a great job," Clancy said, sliding another heated look at Avery.

The server arrived with the sundaes.

"When I gets to kindewgawten, will you make me a costume, Avery?"

"Sure. What would you like to be?"

He flashed her his precious smile. "Fwosty the Snowman."

"I think I can probably handle that."

"Can you make it so I don't melt?"

She grinned. "Absolutely."

They finished their sundaes and headed to Clancy's.

"It's past your bedtime, kids," Clancy said. "Get your jammies on and I'll tuck you in."

Since it was an hour past their bedtime, and they were visibly drooping, he got no argument.

"Can Avery tuck us in, too?" Jett asked when he came to tell his dad he was ready for bed.

"Sure," Clancy said. He pulled Avery up off the sofa and she accompanied him down the hall.

Once the kids were in bed, and he was certain they were asleep, he guided her to his bedroom. He closed the door softly behind them and kissed her all the way to the bed. "Thank you."

"For what?"

"For being you." He reached for the hem of her sweater and tugged it over her head. He tossed it on the floor and unhooked her bra.

Avery moaned when he captured her breast in his mouth.

While he suckled her, he managed to unzip her slacks and his hand dove inside, under her panties.

Avery was so hot by then, she came almost immediately.

Minutes later, their clothing littered the floor. Clancy kissed his way from her feet to her mouth and then he nestled himself between her legs and slid inside her.

"Marry me, Avery. Marry me so we can do this whenever we want to."

She moaned, unable to answer as another orgasm claimed her.

His climax came at the same time, and then he collapsed on top of her.

Avery ran her fingers up and down his backside.

Clancy shivered from her touch. "We're so good together. Why won't you say yes?"

Avery would've answered, but she'd dozed off.

Clancy sighed and kissed her lightly on the lips, wishing things were different…and that Avery wasn't so stubborn.

CHAPTER 27

CHRISTMAS SHOPPING & OTHER THINGS

The snow fell and fell for two days, then it stopped for two days, and after that, it snowed for another two days. The roads were a mess and the school district decided to give the kids an early Christmas present, releasing them three days early for their holiday vacation.

Avery had put in a lot of thought regarding what to get Clancy and the kids for Christmas. While she was thinking, he called and asked if he could hire her to watch the kids for the rest of the week. "Sure, but you don't have to pay me."

"I feel like I should," he said. "I pay Mo, you know."

"Mo's a jewelry designer. She probably needs the money. I don't."

"Are you sure?"

"Positive."

"They want to come to your house, so they can play with Twink."

"That's fine."

"I'll drop them off on my way to work in the morning."

"Okay." She waited for him to say more.

"Thanks, Avery. I really appreciate this."

"You're welcome." Avery sighed and would have said goodbye, but the empty sound of him disconnecting assaulted her ears.

She put down her phone and looked around. Aside from Twinkle, how did you entertain kids every day until the weekend, when Clancy had two days off?

Twink got up from his favorite napping spot and nudged her knee. She leaned over to pet him. "We're having company, starting tomorrow."

Twink woofed, then smiled at her.

"I thought you'd find that exciting."

Twink's head bounced up-and-down, then he bounded away, toward the front door.

"They won't be here until morning, Twink."

That didn't seem to bother the golden, who settled into a curl up against the door.

Avery went back to thinking about Christmas presents. She already had her parents and her siblings taken care of. Their gifts were wrapped in festive red-and-green paper, with curly ribbons on top, and nestled under her tree.

If only she could think what to get Clancy, Jett, and Kenzie.

What it boiled down to was that the three of them had all the creature comforts, and Jett and Kenzie had plenty of toys. Clancy had informed her days ago that he'd bought them both the new gotta-haves for Christmas. When she'd asked what those were, he'd smiled and said, "That, my love, you will have to wait and see."

After another hour of considerable thought, she finally figured out what to get the kids. Jett loved brownies. If she put them in a cute, airtight Christmasy container, he'd like that. She squinted, trying to remember which store carried the Christmas penguin she wanted, then it came to her. Plum Street Kitchen Goods. She picked up her phone and called to see if they still had them on the shelf.

"Hold on, please, and I'll check," said the sales clerk. A few moments later, she said, "I have one left. Would you like me to hold it for you?"

"Yes, please."

"When will you be in to pick it up?"

"Today, if the roads are clear enough."

"I know, right? The snowplows are trying their darnedest, aren't they? What's your name, please?"

"Avery Lark."

"Hey! You write game apps, don't you? I play *Kitty Kritters*, and I love it."

"I'm glad to hear that." *Kitty Kritters* had been her first release six years earlier. Good to know someone who was playing it and loved it.

"I look forward to meeting you, Ms. Lark."

"You, too. See you soon."

That settled her gift for Jett. Now for Kenzie. The more she thought, the more she kept going back to her original idea. Kenzie could sing, but she also liked to draw. "Art supplies it is!" Avery murmured to the empty room.

Twinkle twitched in response, but other than that, had no reply.

Avery checked the clock, which read five minutes after one. If she left now, she could pick up the penguin container, then head to Creek Art Supplies.

That left one person to buy for. Clancy.

Avery smiled. For the man she loved, her gift would be simple. A bow placed strategically on her head should do the trick.

At ten after five on Sunday, her cell phone rang. Sitting at her computer, Avery reached for it, not paying attention to who was calling. "Hello?"

"Aren't you coming for 'sketti night?" Clancy asked.

"Uh, when you called earlier, it sounded like you'd see me tomorrow morning, not this evening." She hesitated, "What's all the racket in the background?"

"Jett's yowling because you're not here and Kenzie's trying to appease him by offering excuses for you."

"Is yowling a word?"

"Please come over, Avery. Your place is already set at the table."

She bit her lip, thinking. Would she have time to finish what she was working on when she came home? Maybe, if she and Clancy didn't visit his bedroom first.

What was she thinking? Of course, they'd visit his bedroom first.

"I'm working, so I need to finish up one thing. I'll be over in a few minutes."

"Good. See you when you get here." He hung up before she could say goodbye.

Four snowmen dotted the O'Rourke's front yard. Three of them had sticks for arms and carrots for noses, but the fourth one was complete with a knit cap and scarf and elaborate sticks for arms, each with mittens dangling at the ends. The face had two rocks for eyes, a carrot for its nose, and six black buttons for its mouth.

Avery pulled out her phone and took a picture, they were so cute.

The front door of the house flew open and Jett and Kenzie ran toward her. They must have remembered what happened before, because they skidded to a halt about a foot away.

"Dinner's getting cold," Kenzie said.

"How come yowa so late?" Jett asked, his arms akimbo, just like his dad often did.

Avery put her phone away and leaned down for a hug. "I was working."

"Working on what?" Kenzie asked.

"A new game app called *Frosties*."

"Is that why you taked a picture of ouwa snowmans?" Jett asked.

"No, I took a picture of them because they're cute. We should get inside. You don't have your coats on."

Before they could respond, Clancy came charging out of the house. He snagged each one of his kids, leaned down and kissed Avery, then turned and headed back into the house.

Inside, which had a slight chill from the front door being left open, he said, "Go wash up."

They two kids grinned up at him and scurried off to the bathroom.

Avery didn't have time to remove her coat before Clancy took her in his arms and kissed the heck out of her.

"Does kissing like that feel good?" Kenzie asked a minute later.

Avery and Clancy pulled apart and Clancy looked down at his daughter, "Yes, it does, and I'd better not see you kissing like that until you're at least thirty."

"I'm only twenty-nine," Avery reminded him.

He turned back to her with a comical expression on his face.

"Let's eat!" Jett screamed, running down the hall from the bathroom.

"Let's do," Clancy said, helping Avery remove her coat. He tossed it on the nearest chair and tugged her alongside him as he strode to the kitchen.

She stalled in the doorway, staring at the table. "Candlelight?" She glanced at Clancy. "What's the special occasion?"

"It's my biwthday week," Jett said. He held up four fingers. "I'm gonna be fowa."

"I didn't know," Avery said, feeling like the odd one out. She pulled free of Clancy's grasp and knelt to hold out her arms to Jett. "If I'd known, I'd have baked a cake." Then it hit her that he'd said it was his birthday week. "What day is your actual birthday?"

He looked at his dad, then back at Avery. "Aftew to-day, fowa mowa days."

"Thursday?"

He nodded with enthusiasm.

"Over dinner, you'll have to tell me what's on your birthday wish list."

"I don't got a biwthday wish list."

"You don't?"

"Uh-uh."

Avery grinned and tapped the end of his nose with a forefinger. "We'll have to continue this conversation later, okay?"

"How much latew?" he asked.

"Tomorrow, when you come to my house?"

"Good. I'll think about what I want."

Clancy scooped him up and set him in his chair, and did the same for Kenzie, then pulled out Avery's chair.

She sat and looked up at Clancy, who smiled and stole another kiss from her.

By seven o'clock, both kids were in bed, fast asleep.

"Care for a nightcap?" Clancy asked.

"Only if you're the nightcap."

He grinned and held out his hand to her. "I was hoping you'd say that."

"I need to leave by nine," she said. "I have a project I absolutely have to finish tonight, since the kids are coming tomorrow."

He nodded and pulled her close. "We'd better not waste any time, then."

Moments later, they were in his bedroom. The door was closed and locked and Avery was discarding her clothes as fast as she could.

Clancy did the same, then reached for her. "You feel so good, Avery."

She reached down to fondle him. "So do you."

He backed her toward the bed. "I want to taste you all over."

"Go for it...."

Clancy wasted no time doing just that.

CHAPTER 28

JETT'S BIRTHDAY

By the time Thursday arrived, Avery had made up her mind about a lot of things.

After extensive conversations with Jett about what he wanted for his birthday, she made no progress toward what to get him, since he kept insisting that all he wanted was to spend the day with her.

Finally, she settled on one thing he could look at throughout his life—an uncirculated silver quarter, minted in his birth year. It was protected with a coin cover and she found a frame to put it in that stood on a stand, so he could view both sides of the coin.

When the kids arrived at eight a.m., she already had the chocolate cake baked. Her intention was to let Jett decorate it, with help from Kenzie and her. Twink would be standing by to clean up the floor of any leavings.

"Did I remember to tell you my family's celebrating Jett's birthday at Pizza King?" Clancy asked.

"No."

He shook his head with a rueful grin. "Sorry, my mind's off in a thousand different directions right now."

"We're decorating his birthday cake today."

"You are? I better let Mo know. She was going to pick one up at the market."

"I don't like mawket cakes, Daddy."

"I know, buddy, but Grammy's busy with the party and—"

"Avery's alweady baked my cake."

Clancy glanced at the kitchen table. "I see that, and chocolate cake is your favorite, too." He leaned down and kissed both kids goodbye. "See you at five."

The two little ones hurried over to the kitchen table with Twink.

Avery walked Clancy to the front door. "I hope it's okay that we're decorating Jett's cake."

"It's perfect." He pulled her close to his big body.

For a second, Avery was afraid he'd ask when she was going to say yes to his marriage proposal, but instead, he kissed her. "I might be a few minutes late picking them up."

She nodded. Them? She decided to ask for clarification. "Is the birthday party just for family?"

"Yeah. Didn't I tell you that?"

Her heart sank. She shook her head.

"Maybe next year, he can have a party with kids." He opened the door and stepped out.

Usually, Avery would have watched him until he rounded the house to the driveway. On this particular morning, she closed the door softly behind him, locked it, and headed back to the kitchen.

Kenzie's coat was tossed over a bar stool and Jett still had his on. She helped him take it off and picked up Kenzie's, hanging them on hooks in the mudroom.

When she returned, they were studying the table. "What's all this stuff?" Jett asked.

"It's for decorating your cake," Avery said.

"What about fwosting?" Jett asked.

"It's frosting, remember?" She'd been working with him all week, hoping to help him speak words with R in them correctly.

Jett nodded and said, "Frosting."

"Excellent, Jett!" Avery gave herself a mental lecture. Not being included in Jett's birthday party wasn't the end of the world, so get over it. "We need to discuss what kind of frosting you like. What's your favorite?"

"Chocolate or the white kind."

"If we do the white kind, do you like the marshmallow kind best, or the sweet fluffy kind, or the kind that comes out of a can?"

"Does the sweet fluffy kind have little mountains?"

"Sure." Why not? She had a cookbook and the world was her oyster. She grabbed her Italian desserts cookbook and searched the index for frostings, then turned to that page. To her surprise, a photo of a cake with Italian meringue frosting was featured.

"That's it!" Jett cried, clapping his little hands.

Avery read the directions, satisfied that she had all the ingredients. "Have you two had breakfast?"

"No," Kenzie said, frowning. "Daddy was in a big hurry this morning."

"It just so happens, I have Corn Pops and blueberry yogurt. How does that sound."

"Yaaaaay!" Jett screamed.

"Delicious!" Kenzie agreed.

While they ate, Avery assembled the Italian icing. It required the stove and the mixer, but by the time Jett and Kenzie were through eating their second bowl of cereal-and-yogurt, the cake was ready to be frosted.

"I never had a square cake a'fore," Jett said.

"I hope that's okay," Avery said, applying the frosting, to which she'd added green food coloring.

"It is! How are we gonna decorate it?"

"Since you were a dragon for Halloween, I thought we

could do dinosaurs for your birthday."

"I love dinosaurs!" He looked around. "Where are they?"

Avery pointed toward the sink. "I washed all of them, so they'd be ready to go on your birthday cake."

Jett jumped out of his chair and ran to the counter, where he could almost see the dinos on the clean dishtowel.

Avery lifted him, so he could have a better look.

"Kenzie, come see! Avery got dinosaurs for my cake!"

Kenzie came running. "Wow! Will you bake my birthday cake, too, Avery?"

"Sure. When is it?"

"April thirtieth."

"That's close to mine."

"When's that?"

"May second."

"Maybe we can have our birthdays together."

"Maybe we can," Avery said, though she wasn't sure Clancy would like that idea. "Bring your bowls and spoons over to the sink. As soon as I rinse them, we can start decorating."

Two hours later, the cake was done.

"Wow!" Jett said. "This is the best cake I ever had."

"It's perfect," Kenzie said.

"I love you, Avery," Jett said again. "Thank you for making my cake!"

"You're welcome, Jett." She grinned down at them. "This was really fun, wasn't it?"

They nodded enthusiastically.

"We'd better get it in the fridge."

"Grammy and Grampy are gonna love my cake," Jett said, laying his head on his folded arms, eyeing the cake with what looked like adoration.

"Auntie Mo and Auntie Tabby, too," Kenzie added. "And Uncle Jace!"

Avery picked up the cake, which she'd put on an oversize cutting board covered with dinosaur paper and clear plastic wrap. "Kenzie, will you open the fridge, please?"

Kenzie ran over to the refrigerator and pulled the door open. The second shelf had been cleared for the cake.

"Thank you. Why don't you guys go watch *Mickey Mouse Clubhouse* while I clean up the mess?"

"We should help you," Kenzie said, studying the table.

"There's not that much to do, sweetie. I can handle it lickety-split."

Jett grabbed her around the knees. "I love you so much, Avery."

"I love you, too, Jett, and you, too, Kenzie." She held out her arm to Kenzie and they had a group hug.

Clancy rang the doorbell at ten minutes after five. Kenzie and Jett ran to let him in.

"Daddy," Jett screamed. "You should see my cake!"

"I bet it's beautiful," Clancy said.

"It is! It is!" Jett grabbed his hand, trying to get him inside. "Come see!"

"I'll see it later, buddy. We need to go home and change clothes, or we're going to be late for your party."

"But…." Jett broke off, apparently hurt that his father didn't want to see his cake.

"Get your coats."

"They're right here," Avery said, feeling a little glum. She handed them over and the kids tugged them on.

"Let's go," Clancy said.

"Wait!" Avery said. "What about the cake?"

"We'll get it when we come back to get you." His hot gaze raked her body.

Avery got all tingly inside. "I thought this was a family-only birthday party."

"It is," Clancy confirmed, then his expression registered that he'd been remiss in making himself clear. "You're part of our family now, Avery."

"I am?"

He nodded and stepped inside, heading straight for her. He pulled her into his arms and kissed her. "We'll be back in half an hour."

Slightly dazed by the intensity of his kiss, she nodded.

Thirty mintes later, the doorbell rang. Clancy stood on her stoop, smiling at her. "I'll carry the cake."

She nodded and turned toward the kitchen. Before she could open the fridge, Clancy said, "Grammy and Grampy are taking the kids tonight and I have tomorrow off."

Avery blinked at him. "You do?"

He nodded, as if waiting for her to say something.

"What about your parents' Christmas party?"

"What about it?"

"Are Kenzie and Jett invited?"

He gave her an odd look. "Of course."

"Oh."

"About tonight?"

"What about it?"

"Your place or mine. You choose."

"You have a bigger bed, and I have a dog."

"You're welcome to bring him along, but he can't get in bed with us."

She shook her head at his silly response. "The only person I want to be in bed with is you."

"Ditto for me." He pulled her into his arms and kissed her again. When he let her go, he said, "The cake?"

Avery opened the fridge door and pulled it open, standing back, so she wasn't in his way.

"My God," he said, staring at it like it was a culinary masterpiece. "You didn't tell me you're a cake decorator, too."

"I'm not," she said, "but the Internet has a wealth of ideas, and I took advantage of them."

Clancy looked as if he wanted to say more, but for some reason, he kept quiet.

Avery closed the fridge door and pulled on her coat. "I'm a little nervous about spending time with your family."

"Don't be. They're all friendly like Mo, and they already love you."

She picked up her purse and Jett's birthday present and headed to the front door, which she opened for him.

Clancy looked down at her. "I can hardly wait for later, Avery."

She smiled to let him know she felt the same way.

Clancy was right. She loved his family, and they loved her.

The cake drew all kinds of compliments, which resulted in questions about the faux boulders, the dinosaur grass, and the frosting. "The kids helped," she said, "and except for the dinosaurs, it's completely edible."

"What does edible mean, Avery?" Jett asked.

"It means you can eat everything except the dinos."

He grinned. "Grammy can wash them for me and I'll play with them at her house."

"Holy cow!" Mike said. "I just realized Jett's using *R*s in his words."

"Avery helped me," Jett said, beaming. "She said since I was four, it was time to say my words correctly." He spoke slowly, which showed he really was trying to get everything right.

"Playing with dinosaurs sounds like fun, Jett," Grampy said. "We can pretend we're in Jurassic Park."

"Yaaaaay!" Jett screamed.

Avery caught Clancy's eye, hoping she hadn't overstepped.

He mouthed, *Thank you.*

She mouthed back, *You're welcome.*

Kenzie said to Avery, "Auntie Mo and Auntie Tabby are taking me Christmas shopping while Jett plays with his dinosaurs."

"That sounds like fun," Avery said, giving her a wink. "Happy shopping,"

Kenzie grinned and winked back. "We asked Uncle Jace to come along, but he said he already has all his Christmas shopping done."

Avery glanced at Clancy's brother.

"Amazon loves me," Jace said, laughing.

Ninety minutes later, they all left the Pizza King.

Jett gave Avery a sloppy kiss and Kenzie managed one that wasn't. "See you tomorrow at the party, Daddy."

"You sure will," Clancy said, hugging his son.

If Avery wasn't mistaken, he had a tear in his eye.

Clancy reached for his daughter next. "'Bye, Kenzie."

"'Bye, Daddy." She whispered in his ear, "Is Avery having a sleepover?"

Clancy grinned. "I hope so."

Kenzie gave him a exuberant hug. "I hope she says yes, this time. Me and Jett want her for a mommy really, really bad."

He set Kenzie back on her feet and glanced at Avery. "Me, too, sweet pea."

"Have you decided yet?" Clancy asked as he drove away from Pizza King.

"We have to go to my place first, to get Twinkle."

"You might want to get a change of clothes, too."

"I might." She slid a look at him, "unless we stay at my place, in which case, you might want to help me undress."

He grinned. "I'm game for that." He reached for her hand.

Every cell inside her body screamed for more of Clancy's touch.

"I bought a new box of condoms."

"I bought a box, too." She shrugged. "The problem is, I can't remember where I put them."

Clancy laughed

Ten minutes later, they pulled up in her driveway.

"Do you want to park in the garage?"

"Is there room?"

"Sure. The left side is mostly empty."

He nodded. "I'll open the door."

"I'll do it," she said, pointing to keypad mounted on the surround."

He leaned over to kiss her. "You're always thinking, aren't you?"

"Not always, but I try." Avery climbed out and went to the keypad while Clancy backed up and lined his SUV up with the vacant side of the garage. The door started to rise. She hurried inside once it was up and he eased into the garage. After he'd parked and turned off the engine, she hit the garage door-opener and the door lowered.

Clancy advanced on her like a panther on the prowl for something delicious. He climbed the two steps and kissed her again.

"Let's get inside," she whispered. "It's cold out here." She turned and opened the door. Twinkle greeted them doing a doggie four-step. "Let me get him some dog biscuits. That'll keep him happy for a while." She hung her coat on a hook in the mudroom.

Clancy hung his, too, and followed her into the kitchen, where she pulled the doggie treats out of a bottom cupboard.

She handed one over to Twink and set the other one on a bar stool, which was within easy reach for the dog.

Clancy scooped her into his arms and carried her down the hallway, kissing her.

"I thought we were never going to make love again," she said in between kisses.

"Why would you think that?"

"You've been so distant lately."

"It's work," he breathed against her neck. "Louise spends so much time at home with Carl, it's doubling my workload." He nipped at her ear. "God, Avery, I've been thinking about this all day."

Avery had, too, but her thoughts had been gloomy, believing they'd never make love again.

He released her and she slid down his body. They tore off each other's clothes like two crazed lovers who hadn't seen each other for years. When they were finally naked, Avery took time to pull back the bedspread, the blanket, and the top sheet, and then she climbed up into the bed and opened her arms to Clancy.

"There's so much I want to do to with you, Avery."

"We have all night," she said, then added dramatically, "Do with me what you will."

After he'd made her come, he worked his way further up her body, tasting her breasts and nipples, and then he kissed her.

"I want you inside me, Clancy."

He reached for the condom packet.

She stayed his hand. "Not tonight."
He was so hot for her, Clancy didn't question why.
Instead, he simply let nature take its course.

CHAPTER 29

CLANCY'S DAY OFF, PLUS SOME

While it took Clancy longer to recover, he made good use of the time by pleasuring Avery.

She lost track of how many orgasms she'd had over the past few hours. All she knew for certain was that she loved Clancy and she wanted to spend the rest of her life with him doing this, and a lot of other things.

If only that three-letter word would pop out of her mouth next time he asked her to marry him.

Around nine a.m., Clancy fondled her breasts. Spooned together, she felt his erection pressing against her derrière.

"Want to try something different?" he asked.

"How much more can there be?" she asked, so sated, she thought she might melt into a puddle of happiness.

He laughed softly. "Kitchen. Garage. Laundry room."

"There's a dog in the house."

"He'll wish he had a doggie girlfriend."

"You should buy the kids a dog."

"Maybe they're getting one for Christmas." His hand slid down over her belly and found her sweet spot.

"This feels so…decadent," she murmured, enjoying what he was doing.

"I want you to come again, sweetheart."

His enticement sent her over the edge. Avery screamed and moaned and mewled as the orgasm hit.

"So good," he said, encouraging her.

Avery twitched and jerked, and finally, she opened her eyes and met his gaze. "I love you, Clancy."

"I love you, too, Avery. So goddamned much it's practically killing me."

At three o'clock, they climbed out of bed and wandered into the kitchen, stark naked.

Twink ignored them, happy to be napping in his bed in the mudroom.

Clancy opened the fridge. "Are you hungry?"

"Only for you."

He laughed softly.

Avery looked down just as his mouth closed over the tip of her breast. "Are you hungry?"

"Only for you, love."

She smiled.

"Forget food," he said. "My folks will have plenty to eat at the party tomorrow night."

He closed the fridge door and carried her to the bathroom, where they showered together and had another wall-banger.

"We should probably eat something," Avery said hours later, studying the contents of her refrigerator.

"I'm happy with tasting you."

She turned and offered him a sexy smile. "I'd like that,

too, but man cannot live on sex alone."

"It's not sex, Avery. I mean it is, but with us, it's making love."

She turned and pressed against him. "I figured you knew what I meant."

"We could do it again, instead of eating."

She nodded and the next thing she knew, they were back in her bed. A few moments after that, he put his hand on her breasts, then his mouth. "You taste so damned good."

"You taste good, too," she murmured, dragging his head up so she could kiss him again.

Avery was so sated, she wasn't sure she could talk, but she had to know when Clancy had to be home for the kids.

"The folks texted that they decided to keep them all weekend," he whispered against her shoulder.

She started. "What about the party tonight?"

He started. "You made me forget about the rest of the world, including my parents' party."

"It starts at seven, right?"

He nodded, nuzzling her breasts.

"It's five now."

He nipped the tip of her left breast, then laved it.

"If you go home now, we'll both have time to get ready."

"We could call and say something came up."

"Gee," she said, her tone dry, "I doubt they'd be able to figure that one out."

He grinned. "We have time to do it again."

"You won't get an argument out of me."

"Good."

Avery repositioned herself. One leg was bent and the other tilted to the side.

"Is that an invitation?"

"It could be."

He smiled that sexy smile of his and nibbled his way down to her toes, then back up to her mound. "Aren't you tired?"

"No, are you?"

"Hell, no. With you, I could do this all day long, every day."

"You'd be broke, if you spent that much time making love with me."

Clancy flashed her a self-satisfied grin.

"Are you hungry?"

"What can we eat, if we're going to pig out later?"

"Not each other."

That made him laugh.

"Let's shower and get ready to go."

"We'd better shower separately, or we'll never make it to the party."

She nodded, wishing the party was a week or two away.

The O'Rourke's party was a rousing success. Avery and Clancy arrived late and left early because the Grands were keeping Kenzie and Jett another night.

Avery rolled over in bed and opened her eyes, expecting to find the man she loved lying next to her.

He wasn't.

She raised up on her elbows and surveyed the room. There he was, sitting in the chair over by the window. "What are you doing?"

"Watching you sleep. You're so damned beautiful, it staggers me."

"I'm not beautiful."

"Look at yourself in the mirror again, Avery."

Avery knew she was passable, but beautiful? No way. "Beauty is in the eye of the beholder."

Clancy smirked. "You have it your way, I'll have it mine, and haven't we already had this discussion before?"

She nodded. "I have something to tell you, Clancy."

"Can it wait? I have a big horny on for you."

"I have a big horny on for you, too." She climbed out of the bed and moved over to the chair, looking down at him. "Your thingy is sticking straight up."

"That's because it wants to be inside you."

"I'd like that."

"We'd both like that." He sighed. "What did you want to tell me?"

She moved closer. "It can wait."

"Good things come to those who wait, huh?"

"I hope so." She extended her hand to him.

In one swift move, he sprang from the chair and picked her up, carrying her to the bed. "Beautiful," he said, staring down at her. Then he eased himself down on top of her and took them both on a ride that left them breathless.

Sunday morning, Clancy rolled off of Avery, his breaths coming hard. He flung an arm over his face.

Avery reached over and ran her fingers over his chest, tweaking his nipples, then going lower and back up again.

"I swore I wasn't going to ask you again, Avery, but my mind, my tongue, my junk, and my heart are all in sync at this moment, so I'm going to anyway." He lifted his arm and met her gaze. "Will you please marry me?"

CHAPTER 30

WILL SHE OR WON'T SHE?

Clancy closed his eyes, awaiting the inevitable *no*.

"Clancy?"

"What?"

"Look at me."

"I can't," he said, his voice sounding agonized.

"I can't give my answer to a man who won't look at me."

Clancy expelled a long, deep sigh.

A moment later, the bed moved, and a moment after that, Avery straddled his groin. His eyes popped open. "What are you doing?"

"Getting your attention."

He gritted his teeth. "Okay, you have it."

"My answer is…."

"For God's sake, Avery, put me out of my misery, once and for all."

"Yes."

"You know I can't take much more of…." His eyes widened. "Did you just say yes?"

She nodded, lowering herself.

He hands snaked out to grab her hips. "Did you really say you'd marry me?"

"I really did."

"What made you change your mind?"

"I have no idea. I wanted to say *yes* from the get-go, but my mouth wouldn't cooperate with my heart."

"Can we get married right away?"

"How soon?" she wanted to know, enjoying what was happening between them.

"Next Saturday?"

"Okay."

"Don't you have stuff to do?"

"I've already thought things through. Kenzie can be my maid of honor, and she'll wear her red dress, with or without the Christmas mini-lights. I bought an incredible red dress to wear, too, if you don't mind that it's not white. You and Jett can wear tuxedos with red cummerbunds. Oh, God, Clancy, what you do to me...." She moaned and threw her head back.

Clancy took the opportunity to raise his hands to her breasts. "We're going to have a great life together, love."

"I know we will...." She moaned as her orgasm hit and just kept coming. Her body twitched and squirmed.

Clancy came at the same time.

Twenty minutes later, Avery said, "There's something else I need to tell you."

"Okay." His hand moved up-and-down her torso, lingering on her abdomen.

"I think...." God, this was going to be harder than she thought.

"You think what?"

"I think I may be...." She sucked in a deep breath.

"You think you may be what, love?"

"I think I may be pregnant."

Clancy offered her a big smile. "Really?"

"Really. I missed my period."

"That makes me really happy."

She stared at him as if he had two heads.

"Don't look at me like that."

"We're not even married."

He splayed his hand across her abdomen. "No, but we will be."

She stared at him, speechless. "You still want to marry me?"

"Of course!"

"Are you sure? I mean, I don't want you to think I tricked you into it, or anything."

"Since I asked you weeks and weeks ago," he reminded her, "I don't think that's a problem."

"Well, yeah, but…."

"No buts, Avery. I love you. You love me. We're meant to be together until the day we die and beyond. We'll have more kids, and a slew of grandkids, and we'll live happily ever after."

"You seem so sure."

"I'm a pragmatist, love. I had a bad marriage, but I got two beautiful kids out of it. Those kids happen to love you, too, and they ask me constantly why you won't say yes to my marriage proposal."

"I can't believe they even know you asked me."

"Walls have ears, love."

"I've heard that before."

He smiled and stroked her cheek. "Now that we have your possible pregnancy kind of figured out, did you find a box on your porch a while back?"

"I did. OMG, I forgot all about it!" She narrowed her eyes on him. "Did you put it there?"

"Yes. Where is it?"

"In the garage. I was afraid to open it because there's

no return address, and no postmark."

"Let's go get it." He jumped out of the bed, pulling her along with him.

"Clancy!"

"Come on. You won't be sorry, I promise."

"We're naked."

His gaze raked her body. "All we're going to do is grab the box."

"You grab it and I'll wait in the doorway. It's cold in the garage."

He laughed and tugged her down the hallway. At the door leading into the garage, he gave her a quick kiss before he opened it. In less than fifteen seconds, he was back with the box. He set in on the washer. "Open it."

Avery grabbed a pair of scissors out of the top drawer and used them to cut the packaging tape. She folded back the box flaps and peered inside, then looked up at Clancy, grinning. "A pregnancy test. How sweet of you to think of it."

"You can use it today, if you want." He grinned. "Just to confirm."

She stared up at him.

He kissed her again. "There's something else in there, too."

Avery stuck her hand back in the box and felt around. Next to the pregnancy test, she felt something small and hard hidden in the tissue paper. She pulled it out and peeled away the tissue. Inside was a red velvet box. She opened it with shaky fingers. "Oh, Clancy," she whispered. "It's beautiful."

"I hope you like it."

"I do." She threw her arms around his neck and kissed him.

"If you don't…."

"I love it. Will you put it in my finger?"

He nodded and removed the two-carat diamond from

it's nest. "I hope it's the right size, but the jeweler said he can size it, if it's not." He slid it on her ring finger.

"I've never seen anything so beautiful."

"It'll never be as beautiful as you."

Avery held out her hand and wiggled her fingers. The beautiful square-cut diamond set in gold sparkled like crazy. She looked up at Clancy. "Are you okay with a ceremony that's simple?"

"Absolutely."

"Just your family and my family and that's it?"

"Yes." He shook his head. "Do you have to question everything?"

"I only do it if I'm not sure about something."

"Don't be not sure about us."

"That," Avery said, "is the one thing I'm absolutely positive about."

"Good. Next Saturday. We'll get married at the folks' house—either yours or mine—and they can keep the kids while we have a sexy honeymoon at my house."

"Who'll take care of Twink?"

"You're impossible."

She grinned. "Isn't that why you love me?"

AUTHOR NOTE

Last year, when I wrote *Yule Loge*, I decided that as the twelfth book in the series, it was time to stop writing Christmas Valley Romances and start a new series. That spawned Sugar Plum Creek Holiday Books, which, as you can imagine, will feature stories that take place during different holidays over the year.

Merry Witchy Christmas is the first of those books, which is a nod to Christmas, primarily, and Halloween, secondarily. Don't worry, I'll have a first-nod to Halloween eventually, because I plan to have eleven more books in this series over the next few years.

Some of the books will have kids and some won't, but my intent is to make them all light-hearted reads. I like including kids and dogs in my books, especially because they can add an amusement element to the story. If you laughed and smiled your way through *Merry Witchy Christmas*, then my goal was accomplished.

Many, many thanks to my editor, Nancy Jankow, for *all* her helpful comments. The rewrites Nancy suggested made this a much better book. *Grazie, mia amica!*

I hope all of you have a happy and joyful holiday season! Watch for *Stupid Cupid*, coming in February 2023. Jennie has a life-changing event in that book, and when she meets Cyrus, well, you can imagine how that's going to go....

Merry Christmas, happy holidays, and happy reading!

THANK YOU!

Thank you so much for reading
MERRY WITCHY CHRISTMAS!
I'd love to hear what you think about it.
You can email me at **ann@annsimas.com**, or post a
comment on my **Ann Simas, Author** page on
Facebook. I hope you'll "like" me while you're
there, and if you are so inclined,
please leave a review on
Amazon.com or Goodreads.com.
You can also find me on BookBub.com.

JUST FOR FUN

If would like to submit a picture of yourself reading
this or any book by me, please send your JPG to
ann@annsimas.com
and I'll post it on my FAN page!

SANTA'S HELPER
Christmas Valley Romances #1

Page forward for a preview.

Chapter 1

Sean D'Arcy propped his size elevens up on the desk, leaned back in the executive chair, and commenced tapping his gold Cross pen against the leather-clad arm. December 10 and he hadn't bought a single present for anyone on his Christmas gift list.

"Tick-tock," he muttered. He swung his feet to the floor and threw down the pen in disgust. His six-foot-two frame came up out of the chair, dwarfing the room. His list was started, but when the hell was he supposed to find time to go out and *buy* everything? How had he managed it in years past? Why was his time this year stretched so thin?

Sean checked his watch. Coincidentally, his stomach rumbled and he realized it was an hour past noon. He pulled out his wallet to make sure he had some cash, or at least some bills small enough to feed into the change tender. Four Franklins, one Grant, and one Jackson. Ever the optimist, he headed to the employee lounge in hopes someone could break the twenty.

Most of the employees who worked the administrative end of D'Arcy Implements took lunch between 12:00 and

1:00, but Janelle Fridley, his CFO, had a spreadsheet and her lunch spread out on the largest round table in the room. She devoured both with equal fervor.

"Hey, Jani," Sean greeted her. "Can't you read a paperback on your lunch hour like a normal person?"

Janelle glanced up at him with a rueful grin. "What can I say? I'm in love with your company financials, Sean. Every day, they keep me enthralled."

Sean shook his head. Those increasing numbers were probably why he hadn't had time to Christmas shop, something he'd loved doing since forever. Come to think of it, he hadn't been doing anything extracurricular for far too long. "Lucky for me you know your numbers."

"Lucky for me, you have a head for business."

"You two make a great mutual admiration society," cracked Brian Crane, the company risk manager. He dumped some quarters into the snack machine.

Sean laughed. "Can either of you break a twenty?"

"Deb cleaned out my wallet this morning," Brian said. "All I have is loose change."

Janelle dug into the purse hanging by a strap from the back of her chair. "I can front you a fiver."

He tried to give her the twenty in exchange.

She shook her head. "I trust you."

"Thanks. How come no one has cash these days?"

Brian opened a package of crackers. "Plastic, buddy. Plastic."

Sean fed the five into the change machine. "Then maybe we should get snack and soda machines that take plastic."

"Good idea," Janelle said. "I'll look into it."

Brian left, citing new governmental safety regulations to be read. Janelle went back to her spreadsheet and a piece of string cheese. Munching Cheetos, Sean wandered over to the cork bulletin board. He perused it at least once a week so he could keep abreast of employee activities, both work- and off-the-clock-related. Someone was selling cosmetics for the holidays. Someone else was looking for a babysitter.

"How's the onsite day-care center shaping up?" he asked Janelle.

"That's what I'm working on now. I'll have it on your desk tomorrow, latest. If all goes well, we can have it up and running when we open again in January."

Sean gave her a thumbs-up and went back to reading notices. Someone wanted a fourth for a weekly Pinochle game. Someone else had a few household items to sell.

And then, right there in the middle of the board, an ad that offered Christmas shopping services.

The poster measured about twelve inches square. Though eye-catching, it was obviously handmade. Below the candy-cane striped Santa's Helper heading was a picture of the elf herself. She wore a green cap tilted at a jaunty angle on her mass of lustrous auburn hair. Her green sweater had a little reindeer pin affixed to the cowl neck. Between that cap and the reindeer, sexy green eyes stared back at him.

It wasn't a professional photo, but whoever had taken it had captured something in the elf's expression. Mischief, amusement, and a little something else….

He blinked, then blinked again, but the come-hither invite was still there.

Sean just about choked on a Cheeto.

He leaned forward to examine the photo up close. Finally, his gaze dropped down to read the text below.

Too busy to shop for Christmas?
Leave it to Santa's Helper!
Elf Lily Hammond to the rescue-
And free gift-wrapping, too!
555-5656 or email Lily@santashelper.com
Don't wait: Availability 12.10 – 12.22 only!

Sean glanced at his watch to check the date. Holy shit! Today was the tenth. What if she was booked up already?

He pulled down the poster and moved over to Janelle's

table. "Do you know who put this up?"

Focused on her number-crunching, Janelle was slow to lift her head. Her glance went from his face to the poster in his hand, which rained glitter down on her spreadsheet. "Me?" she responded hesitantly, as if she thought she might be in trouble over it.

"So you know her?"

Janelle nodded.

"Do you know anyone who's used her? I mean, is she any good?" Sean cursed silently. "I mean, to shop."

Janelle sat back in her chair and contemplated him. Her lips twitched. "This is her second season elfing it, and as far as I know, all her clients last year were satisfied."

Sean studied the elf's photo again, trying to figure out why she appealed to him.

Wait! That was stupid. It wasn't the elf who appealed to him. Well, she did, but it was the service she *offered* that he needed. He was busy, she was a shopper. That was it.

Period.

Question mark.

"Is there a problem?"

"No. No!"

"Because Lily's a friend of mine. I thought it would be okay to help her out and I certainly wouldn't have put up the poster if I didn't think she could deliver."

"Of course not."

Sean made his way to the door, his mind running rampant on exactly what Lily could deliver. "I mean, uh, I know you wouldn't post anything bogus."

"She only does this seasonally, to supplement her web business."

With his eyes glued to the photo of the elf on the page, he barely heard his CFO.

"Hey, wait! Are you taking the poster?"

Sean debated for fifteen minutes. Should he call or

email, call or email?

Call.

Email.

He composed an email, read it, rolled his eyes. Deleted it. Composed it again.

He picked up the phone, dialed, disconnected on the sixth digit. Dialed again. Hung up before the first ring.

Picked up the phone again.

Slammed it down.

Picked it up. Slammed it down.

"So, what, you're twelve now, you idiot?"

He went back and reread the email, satisfied that he sounded like a responsible adult and not some teenage boy slobbering over a picture of a hot chick in an elf hat.

He hit SEND before he could change his feeble mind again.

While he stared at the photo of the elf—who, to be fair, really should be calling herself a vixen, not an elf—his computer *pinged*, announcing he had an email.

Dear Sean,
Thank you for your email. I would be delighted to meet with you regarding your Christmas-present shopping needs. I have a 3:00 slot available this afternoon, if that's convenient for you.

Regards,
Lily Hammond
Santa's Helper

Sean hit REPLY and wrote:

Miss Hammond,
3:00 p.m. works for me. I am at 4310 Wausau Place, top floor. I'll let the receptionist know to expect you.

Thank you.
Sean D'Arcy

SEND.

With a sappy grin on his face, Sean leaned back in his chair, poster in-hand, staring at the picture of the elf, Lily Hammond.

His pulse did something weird and his heart might have turned a somersault, which was ridiculous, because Sean D'Arcy, CEO of D'Arcy Implements did not get gooey over women. Women got gooey over him.

He put the poster aside and went to work making a list.

Lily pushed away from her laptop and commenced doing the happy dance around the room. Macey gave her a toothy, drooly grin and lifted her arms. Lily scooped her up. "We got a response, Macey! If Mama gets this job, we might have a teeny-tiny Christmas this year! Won't that be amazing?"

Macey clapped her dimpled little hands together, squealing, "Jinga bell, jinga bell."

Lily nuzzled her daughter's cheek."That's right, baby." They twirled and flounced around the small room to "Jingle Bell Rock."

"Mo', mo'," the toddler demanded when the song had finished. As if on command, Brenda Lee belted out "Rockin' Around the Christmas Tree" and then the CD Jani had made for Macey would start all over again.

Lily and her daughter loved the REPEAT function on her little CD player.

SANTA'S HELPER
Christmas Valley Romances #1

Available worldwide in paperback or as an ebook at
amazon.com

Also available in paperback from
annsimas.com

ABOUT THE AUTHOR

 Ann Simas lives in Oregon, but she is a Colorado girl at heart, having grown up in the gorgeous Rocky Mountains. An avid word-lover since childhood, she loves reading and writing. The author of 40 novels, one novella, and seven short stories, she particularly enjoys writing books that are cross-genre—a mix of mystery/thriller/suspense, with a love story and sometimes, paranormal or supernatural elements.

In addition to being a three-time Romance Writers of America Golden Heart Finalist, Ann is an award-winning watercolorist and budding photographer who enjoys needlework and gardening in her spare time. She is her family's "genealogist" and has been blessed with the opportunity to conduct first-hand research in Italy for both her writing and her family tree. The genealogy research from century's-old documents, written in Italian, has been a supreme but gratifying and exciting challenge for her.

Contact the author at
ann@annsimas.com

Or visit:
annsimas.com *and*
Ann Simas, Author on Facebook
Ann Simas on BookBub.com

Ann's books are available worldwide at
amazon.com

Made in the USA
Middletown, DE
05 October 2022